ROSEWAY

The Road that Never Ends

REBECCA ROBINSON

Scriptures taken from the Holy Bible, New International Version®, NIV®. Copyright © 1973, 1978, 1984, 2011 by Biblica, Inc.™ Used by permission of Zondervan. All rights reserved worldwide.

Author photo taken by Gary Collier, Collier Photo: www.collierphoto.ca

ISBN: 978-1-77069-424-8

Printed in Canada

Word Alive Press
131 Cordite Road, Winnipeg, MB R3W 1S1
www.wordalivepress.ca

ALSO BY REBECCA ROBINSON

When Times Stands Still under the pen name of Rebecca Hickson (Xulon Press 2005) ISBN 1-594677-27-1 Printed in the United States

The Narrow Road Series

Roseway – The Road that Never Ends (Word Alive Press 2012)

Ripley – The Road of Acceptance (Word Alive Press 2012)

Jenn – The Road of Sacrifice (Word Alive Press 2012)

Library and Archives Canada Cataloguing in Publication

Robinson, Rebecca Wills
    Roseway : the road that never ends / Rebecca Wills Robinson.

    I. Title.

PS8635.O2635R68 2011   C813'.6   C2011-907668-3

Contents

ACKNOWLEDGEMENTS

One day I sat with pen and notebook in hand and asked the Holy Spirit to inspire my writing and creativity. I was fresh out of creative writing class when my pen began to flow. This character named Roseway came to life on my pages. Within half an hour, I had written the first chapter. I must first thank the Holy Spirit who gives me the creativity and the inspiration to write these stories which hold many biblical truths. Roseway – The Road that Never Ends is the first book in The Narrow Road series.

I sincerely and with much gratitude thank my friends Anne Acacia and Sue Beadmen, who read through the rough pages and gave me their constructive criticism and advice. Your gentle comments took me back to the revision table.

I would like to also say a special thank-you to Gwendolyn Elliot for editing each book in the *Narrow Road* series line by line and page by page to bring the creativity and the grammatical together in Technicolour.

Many have prayed for me during this writing and publishing process. I know that your prayers have motivated me and encouraged me to continue during times when I felt the ink was going dry. I covet all your prayers.

To the entire Word Alive Press publishing team who each worked on the completion of *Roseway*, I also give a heartfelt thank-you. Keep up the great work in presenting the gospel message to the world through the written word. Tom Buller, I appreciate all your helpful writing tips and final edits. I will improve. Thanks. Jen Jandavs-Hedlin, it has been a pleasure working and conversing with you throughout the entire process.

Thanks to all brave hearts that share their testimonies and tell how God has worked in their lives through a variety of trials, struggles and hardships. Your stories also inspired some of these fictional writings. While all the characters are fictional, so many people can relate to one or two of these life challenges the characters endure. These books will help others find that blessed assurance found in no other source than our Lord Jesus Christ, who gets all the honour, glory and praise. Amen.

PROLOGUE

Running through the trees, Roseway was anxious to get to the old log cabin. She could hardly recognize where it once stood. The overgrown saplings had changed the landscape, making it difficult to find the burned ruins. For twelve years, this place had been her prison and Big Joe her warden. They say time heals all wounds and changes perspectives. Life for Roseway had taken a road she thought would never end. Along that journey, she'd grown from a child to a teenager and then into a young woman.

She stopped and looked at a little grave marking where a small oak tree had sprouted. The sun squeezed through the tall trees, bathing the leaflets. Looking at the tree reminded her of the day she had watched the little acorn fall from a tree and land into its God-appointed place, the day when she'd buried the contents of her shoe into the little grave.

Now, a couple of years later, in spite of all the strong winds which had come and gone, that little tree had reached toward the sunlight and dug its roots to the depths of the underground springs to stand victorious amongst its rivals. In many ways, Roseway felt like she was similar to that little tree. Life made so much more sense now than it had then. A tear collected in the corner of her eyes as she remembered when she first knelt at that grave and watered the wildflower with her tears. At that time, she'd had so many fears and questions—and no answers. What she did have was faith and hope. These were the impetus which guided her through the meadows and along the roadways.

Ripley and Joseph slid down the small hill to meet up with Roseway. They were laughing at each other as they made jokes about Roseway and her excessive determination and speed.

With a big smile planted on his face, Joseph breathlessly blurted, "Where is the fire?" Noticing Roseway's silence and the charred remains of an old cabin poking through the saplings, Joseph realized where they'd ended up. Catching his breath, he gave Ripley a serious look as he noticed the tears streaming down Roseway's face. Joseph put his arm around her, sensitively realizing that she needed this moment to grieve her loss, in her own time and in her own way. Everything in her life had changed, yet the bitter root of all her pain was hidden deep in the memories and ashes of that old cabin.

The sounds of the forest, including the flowing stream in the distance, were heard in the silence. With a sigh, Roseway, looked up at Joseph and said, "I just didn't have the understanding I needed when I lived here with Big Joe. The pieces of the puzzle just didn't fit. Now I have the pieces. Somehow it is still not enough. I was a little girl. My childhood was stolen from me. No matter how much I have gained understanding, it does not change many things."

She looked over at Ripley, who sat quiet and patient with a look of sympathy. Ripley was her constant friend and Roseway felt the security deep within herself. Together they had been to hell and back in the short period of time since they'd first met at that dumpster. Their unspoken conversation was loud and clear. Roseway's glance drifted over to Joseph. His expression was compassionate, supportive, and steadfast. For a moment, she wondered what her life would have been like without them. The answer stared her in the face as she looked over to the field where the cabin once stood. Now the field was filled with wildflowers and saplings. Everything was naturally springing back to life. A revelation awakened in her heart. Some things are best left in the ashes. It is what grows from the ashes that we take with us today and tomorrow. Roseway looked at these two special people in her life. Pointing to the empty field, Roseway broke the silence. "Could I show you a very special place of mine?"

Ripley and Joseph followed Roseway through the bush and over the ridge. Ripley climbed up onto a large rock cliff that had a slight overhang above the flowing stream. The three of them sat there for a moment, watching the water. Roseway began to reminisce. Ripley and Joseph listened as one listening to the flow of a stream, attentive and captivated.

1
ROSEWAY

Roseway sat in a meadow surrounded by endless forest backdropped by mountains with different shades of reds and greens. The natural beauty of the landscape and the serenity flowing in the air captivated her. She was the portrait of a princess. Her eyes lit up with sparkles of marine green within velvet brown. Mahogany hair with silky blond highlights danced in the light, gentle breeze, completing the innocent softness of her face.

Roseway often went to the meadow of tranquility to escape reality. Here, she would seek peace and refreshment. Roseway would remember a Bible scripture her mother had taught her when she was a young child. Whenever she came to the meadow, she recited the verse. It gave her hope that someday soon her Saviour would hear and answer. For many years, Roseway had faithfully said it like a prayer. Something was different about this day.

She began to pray. "The Lord is my Shepherd. I shall not want. He makes me to lie down in green pastures."

With an abrupt silence, she stopped after saying a few lines. This time, her eyes filled with tears of desperation and frustration as she cried out to the Lord.

"Oh Lord, my mind cannot dance. My heart cries with sadness. Where do I go from this place? I'm trapped in a desert, so dry. I thirst for the water of life. I long for you to set me free. Where are you, Lord? Quench this emptiness within my soul. Oh God! Allow me to sense your amazing love. Oh God! Set me free. Rescue me. Rescue me. Oh Lord, please rescue me."

Roseway wept, sobbing until she was tired and weak. She sat numb, dazed, as if her mind was drifting someplace else. Slowly, her eyes gazed at the sight of a little buttercup. It, too, was alone, lost in a meadow of green—set apart in the mass of grass, yellow, bright, and flowering like a garden rose. It was flourishing and brilliant, bringing vitality to the green meadow. The flower entranced her as she watched it peek through the ground and reach to the light-consummating life. Slowly, she reached out her shaking hand to caress its beauty. She tenderly slipped her fingers around the delicate flower. Her face leaned over the flower, trying to breathe a fragrance that would match its beauty. Inhaling the aromaless scent, her face took on a blank expression and a stare of disappointment. She glared at the flower sitting helplessly in the palm of her hand. She closed her hand, smothering the flower. Vengeful anger gripped her knuckles white as she ripped the flower from its stem. Slowly, Roseway opened her clutched fingers and looked at the destruction held in the palm of her hand.

For only a moment, she saw the beauty in the wildflower. Nevertheless, now as she looked at it, she could only see a mirrored image of herself. As she stared, the buttercup fell to the ground.

Feeling like all her hope was gone, Roseway turned and walked away. Shoulders slouched, head looking down, she sauntered through the meadow. She was caught in sorrow—sorrow she had held within her heart for years. Roseway no longer heard the magical music of the singing birds or dancing trees. She only heard the emptiness of her heart echoing through the chambers of her mind. Walking aimlessly, Roseway came to a stream of swiftly moving water. A group of rocks crowded the stream's edge, making it look like an inviting place to rest. She sat on an elevated rock, hunched over, holding her head in her hands, oblivious to the beauty that surrounded her.

A splash of water lunged at her from the swiftly moving current. She ignored the splash but could not ignore the flopping fish that appeared mere feet in front of her—or could she? The fish found itself taken from its home, and was now desperately trying to get back to the water.

Again Roseway sat as if caught in another time and place. Yet her eyes were fixed on the little silver fish flip-flopping, struggling for life. A serene grin came over her face, sympathizing for a moment with the little fish. Somehow she could not find it within herself to get off that rock. Something kept her from freeing the fish back to the water of life. Minutes passed by, and the silver fish lay in the sand. The fish's scales were slowly drying, its gills expanding trying to take a breath. It was dying slowly from lack of water and oxygen, and the hot penetrating sun. Suddenly, Roseway's stare was interrupted. A gripping wave of water crashed over the shore's edge, pulling the little fish back into the water where it disappeared.

Roseway jumped off the rock and rushed to the water to see the fish. The misery that minutes ago had kept her company was now gone. Now all she saw was her reflected image, reminding her again of the decay slowly eating away any love she once carried within her heart. A tear trickled down her round cheek and dripped into the stream, making a ripple that seemed to go on and on.

The sun began to set, cooling the night air. Clouds hid the sun like an overbearing lead blanket of dismal grey. Uncomfortable, wet

3

and cold, she began to make her way home, but where was home? The place she laid her head at night echoed emptiness. Many walls marked the passing years that stood as her foundation, reminding her of the hurt and pain. Memories would invade her thoughts, feeding her anxiety. So many invisible walls were hemming her in, causing her to feel like she was drowning. *How can I continue?*

The darkness of night covered the earth, yet it felt better than daylight. Perhaps it was because in the dark Roseway could no longer see the walls. Treading the path back to the cabin, she dragged every step. She listened intently to the crickets and frogs orchestrating a symphony of music. The stars came out one by one, adding a pleasant glow to the sky's blackness. Roseway almost found pleasure as the face on the moon seemed to smile hopefully at her.

Nearing the rustic cabin, the abode of all her sorrow, she slowed her pace. Then, as she glanced ahead, a spectacle of light lit the path. As she stretched her vision, she could feel the pounding of her heart increase. With nervous suspense she raced forward to see the blaze. Heat combed the cool night air as she quickly approached the remnants of the cabin. As she arrived, she saw it crumble to the ground into ashes. Roseway looked intently to find a glimpse of some refuge. A shadow startled Roseway, then scurried away into the darkness. She wondered if it could possibly be Big Joe. Joe was big and strong with a heart like coal. The site of the fire-red coals slipped her back into another time and place, into a memory of Big Joe. The memory of his big hands and the smell of smoke and whiskey lingered in her senses. Joe had weatherworn skin, rough and scarred. He was an image firmly imprinted in her mind. His sharp hard voice cut like a pirate's blade. Chills of fear, anger and hatred consumed her. Roseway hoped with all her soul that the shadow was just her fearful imagination. She hoped that Joe might be at the bottom of the red-hot coals.

Roseway

A sense of peace came over Roseway for the first time in a long while. Feeling like a chained captive set free, a hope of freedom embraced her. The word freedom to Roseway meant no more walls, no more abuse. Overwhelmed by the aspiration, she wept tears of joy. Emotions of laughter and tears caused her to sob with such release. She gained ignited hope that she could return to the home she had known as a child. Somewhere out there in the big vast world was her real family, from where Joe had stolen her childhood. It was a place she knew as home, where safety, love, and gentleness existed. She was anxious to seek out a way to get there, wherever the place might be. First she had to sit quietly until the ashes cooled, and then have one last look at the remnants of that old cabin of horror. She had to put it to rest.

Late into the next day, the ashes had cooled enough for Roseway to walk into where the entrance door once stood. With the still fresh vision of everything in its place, Roseway entered the cabin area. She envisioned the walls that Joe had once laced with many pictures of her family. For so many years, those pictures represented her only glimmer of hope. A constant reminder of a family she loved so much. It was for this love Roseway endured and suffered. In a way, she laid down her life so they could live. Joe had used the pictures as a threat, dangling them over her head like candy to a child.

Looking through the still hot ashes, Roseway found a half-burned picture. As she looked at it through teary, blurred eyes, she noticed an address on the back. Roseway wiped her eyes with her dirty cuff, then held the picture to her breast. Her only hope was that this address would lead to home. Putting the picture in her pocket, Roseway walked over to where her bed once awaited her.

Roseway reached down into the ash heap again and pulled out a brass belt buckle. It was still hot to the touch. As she flipped it from one hand to the next, she read the imprint on the front. It was a charcoal-stained "J." She was very familiar with the belt buckle. The only time it left Joe's waist was when he used the belt to punish her or when he went to bed. She took off her shoe and placed the buckle in the shoe along with a handful of ashes.

The sunrise was lighting the horizon. Roseway turned to leave and never return. Just then a raspy voice echoed through her mind. *Don't you dare leave or......*Roseway shook her head to make the voice stop, and then kept walking. With one shoe on her foot and the other treasure-filled shoe in her hand, she continued on without looking back.

She walked a couple of miles, feeling more freedom with each passing step. Then she rested under a tall oak tree. While she was sitting beneath the tree, she noticed a little buttercup set apart from any other flowers. Beside it, she dug a little hole and emptied the contents of her shoe. She covered over the hole with soil. Roseway sat and admired the little buttercup, just as she had admired the flowering buttercup days before. This time as she reached down to smell the flower, a tear trickled down her face, rolled off her chin, and landed on the delicate flower. Realizing she had watered the buttercup with her tears, a grin of acceptance came upon her face.

Just as Roseway was about to leave, a gentle breeze began to blow. As she took one last glance at the little grave, an acorn fell from the tall oak tree, landing in the hand-tilled soil. Roseway turned to continue her journey home.

The sun shone brightly down upon her, warming her back. The gentle breeze pushed her forward like a loving arm. For the first time she breathed relief, feeling like everything was okay. She felt like her nightmare was finally over. In her heart she believed she would find her way home, even though she had no idea of how to get there or where home was. A seed of faith had grown within

Roseway's heart. In a meadow of loneliness and desperation, God had heard and answered her humble prayer. There was still a journey set before her, yet she had such peace within. Despite all the horrible things of her past, she had a renewed hope to continue. Roseway's trust in God was growing.

2
THE MEADOW

Long green grass tickled Roseway's legs with each step homeward. The terrain slowly changed to rocks, trees, and hills as she walked out of the green meadow. For a while the sun was warm and the breeze was gentle and soothing. A smile of freedom came upon her face. She could hear the orchestra of creation serenely playing in her ears like a symphony of instruments, coming from all around her. The birds whistled like flutes and the crickets sounded like raindrops falling on the water. The high-pitched cicadas sang like a choir of sopranos and cymbals.

Roseway felt joyful anticipation. Desperately, she clung to the hope of going home. Roseway walked toward her dream, marking a new path with each step. This day, she saw the world with brand new vision. The prison of yesterday seemed miles behind. With the sense of such freedom, she began to run as if on a heavenly cloud. She had no sense of time as she sprinted, for time had not made her a prisoner. Her clock was the sun and the moon. God was her compass. Roseway had shoes on her feet and the clothing on her back. No bag slung over her shoulder. All she had was an old worn picture with an address written on the back, tucked gently in her breast pocket.

Living in a cabin in the bush all these years, Roseway had learned some survival skills. Often, Joe would send her out to pick wild mushrooms, certain weeds like char, edible plants, and berries. Throughout the day she traveled, eating the sparse food she could find. Roseway began to feel tired and thirsty. Bushes of Sumac lined the path beside a swiftly moving stream. She picked some of the dark red fruit from the tree, trying to drink some of its bitter juice. The stream was a haven for her to rest. Swallowing the dry lump in her throat, she ran to the stream with a life-filled smile lighting up her face. The water was a refreshing gift. Roseway plunged her little hands into the water and put her face close, drinking with such thirst. She splashed her face and danced with joy, feeling like a child again. Then she looked down at the water and once again saw her reflection. This time, she did not feel so alone. For a moment, she could recognize a little hope and a little more acceptance of herself. But still there was something missing in that picture. Emptiness lingered within her eyes. Though she knew in her mind that God was near, her world was like a deserted island.

Roseway gasped in surprise as she saw that little silver fish from days before, looking up at her. The little fish skimmed the top of the water, fluttered its gills for only a moment, and then turned and swam downstream. Roseway watched until it was out of sight. She took seeing the silver fish again as a sign from God that she was going in the right direction.

The silver fish also reminded her of a memory: the first time she went fishing with Big Joe. *He took her by her little hand as they walked close to the stream. In his other hand he had a fishing pole. Big Joe cast the line into the water. He bent down and told Roseway to hold the fishing rod for him while he went to bait another rod. He said to Roseway, "When ya feel a liddle tug on da end of da rod, give it a ard pull back and reel in da fish."*

Before a few seconds had past, the fishing rod began to bend. Doing exactly what Big Joe had told her to do, she pulled hard on the fishing rod and reeled as quickly as she could. The rod bent and the fishing line tightened as the fish on the other end fought back. The excitement she felt making the catch was exhilarating. Roseway felt she had just done an amazing thing. Then Big Joe took the fish off the hook and threw it back in the water. "Dat fish is too small, we best trow it back in da water and catch it when it gets a liddle bigger." They fished all that day. Big Joe cooked up a couple of his big fish on the fire. Then, after supper, they headed back to their cabin.

She had forgotten that memory until then. For a moment, it stirred some new feelings. Roseway scratched her head, turned and began to search for branches.

This seemed like a good place to make a small shelter as the sun was beginning to set. With the fallen, weathered trees, Roseway built a small lean-to up against a big rock. She overlaid the walls with reed mats that she made by weaving pieces of birch bark together with a spruce root. With spruce gum, she then sealed the seams. The ground cedar and sturdy branches were enough to cover any holes in the walls and roof. As she worked, some of the small pieces of cedar and leaves fell through the cracks, making her a bed.

Darkness began to creep into the air as the sun set behind the horizon. Putting the last branches on the fort, she heard a growl from amongst the trees. Slowly she looked behind her and made eye contact with a wolf, but then quickly looked to the ground as not to accept a challenge. With a stick in hand, she began hitting the ground in warning.. The wolf continued to move slowly around her camp, continuing with an inquisitive stare that Roseway respectively engaged with only a glance. Roseway felt the beat of her heart swoosh in her ears. Fear braced her for a few moments. As they continued in the dance, the wolf marked his territory. Then he raised his head high and howled like a French horn. As quickly as he had appeared, he then vanished into the forest. Relaxing, Roseway entered securely into her fort. Exhausted, she curled herself up like a snail.

The cool night air and the dampness from the ground seeped into her bones. *If only I had a blanket,* she thought. The wind from the blowing trees seemed to be raging in battle, thrashing their branches back and forth as if fighting off some invisible evil. The sound of the moving stream flushed over the shore's edge in a roar. Howling in the near distance was a pack of wolves. She poked her head out of the entrance of the door for a moment, to take one last look around. The moon's reflection lit up their fluorescent eyes. Evil-looking stares encamped all around the fort. They looked like stars in the black of night. Were they a deceptive figment of her worst imagination or were they watching over her? She wondered, as she closed the door to the fort tight. With each sound louder than the one before, Roseway fought to keep awake as her eyes crossed with tiredness. Just as she started to relax, the rustle in the leaves beside her fort restrained her sleep. She pulled the cedar foliage over top of her body, trying to find some warmth. The harsh sound of Joe's voice still haunted her in the darkness of the night. In fear, Roseway curled herself up in a foetal position and began to pray herself to sleep. *Oh Lord, please make it go away. Protect me through the night.*

Morning finally arrived with the warmth of the rising sun heating the fort like a warm fire. Roseway awoke to singing birds to face a new day. She bathed herself in the stream, dressed and smiled with victory, and continued to walk her journey home. Of the hundreds of different species of mushrooms, Joe had taught her which ones were poisonous and which were edible. Along the way, she stopped and picked a few mushrooms and green plants for breakfast. It was enough food to keep her going.

After traveling many days and miles through the forest, Roseway came to a roadway. She did not know where the road would take her. Standing there looking down the long road, it seemed to go on forever. She was tired and hungry. Somehow she had fantasized walking out of the forest and finding her little white house with Billy, Suzie and Momma standing there waiting. Instead, all she'd found was a long road ahead of her. She chose a direction and walked down the road for hours. Only one car sped by her. She tried to chase it down until she was exhausted. Frustrated, with feelings of helplessness, tears began to well up in her eyes, then anger. She yelled to God. "Now what am I supposed to do?" Her hope and faith were beginning to dwindle. She picked up a stone, threw it as far as she could and let out a loud, bottomless scream. She kicked the dirt, stomped the ground and then sat in her despair and cried. It was hours of waiting before a transport truck came along. The air brakes made a loud swish as the truck came to a stop in front of her. Roseway stood, feeling so tiny as she looked up at the monster of a truck. She didn't remember ever seeing anything so big and intimidating. The big white door opened.

The man inside the truck said, "Hello, what is a young woman like you doing way out here? Would you like a ride?"

For a moment, Roseway hesitated. It was as if a spacecraft had landed and this strange alien from another planet was speaking Martian to her. Roseway rubbed her neck as it kinked from looking up. With her other hand, she dusted off her pants and wiped the dust from her eyes. She pondered, feeling pulled from all sides. *Should I get in the truck? What if he is just like Joe? What choice do I have? Where I am going?* Not knowing whether to run the other way or get in the truck, she followed her desperation. She half-smiled with uncertainty as a feeling of relief crept into her soul, transforming the expression on her face. *This has to be an answer to prayer,* she convinced herself. Timidly, she said, "I would appreciate a ride very much." Roseway eased her way into the truck.

The truck driver continued to speak as they drove down the road. "By the way, my name is Joe. What is your name?"

3
THE HAND PRINT

Roseway's eyes opened wide and her face took on an expression of fear. Her hand reached for the door handle, while her leg edged nervously away from Joe. She contemplated jumping out of the quickly moving truck.

"So, what is your name?" Joe asked, trying to strike up a conversation. Roseway sat as if trapped in a frozen cocoon. "Does the cat have your tongue? I've been driving for three hundred miles without any conversation. You know, driving can get very quiet and boring when you're all by yourself. Back home, I have a sister about your age. Her name is Gabrielle. Sometimes she comes on short trips with me to keep me company. My name is actually Joseph. A nice biblical name, don't you think? My mother always liked the bible story about Joseph. Do you know that story?" Roseway still sat quiet. "I guess that story about Joseph was always an encouragement to my Mom. We've had many struggles in life, but always trusted the Lord to provide. The story of Joseph being cast out from his family and then imprisoned, only to someday become as powerful as a king; it just shows you, if you trust in God, He can save you from any circumstance. Sorry, I guess I'm rambling on."

Joseph was a young, handsome man in his early twenties. His black hair was shiny, trimmed neatly around his ears. He had big brown eyes, a slender nose, and an olive complexion. He looked nothing like Big Joe. Joseph's pleasant appearance and gentle tone of voice eased Roseway's hesitation to communicate. His smile lit up his face, teeth straight and white—almost too perfect looking, unlike big mean, toothless Big Joe. His bible story hit a soft chord. Roseway's eyes began to brighten with the realization of her new-found freedom.

"My name is Roseway," she responded in a cautious, mellow tone. "I'll call you Joseph, if you don't mind? I don't much like the name Joe."

"Well at least you are honest. I must say, I have never heard a name like Roseway. That is a different name. Why did your Mom call you Roseway?"

Sullenly she replied. "My Mom named me Rose because roses are her favourite flowers. The first time she held me in her arms, the baby smell was so sweet. When she looked at me, she said you are my little Rose. At least that is what she once told me."

"Well, Rose, where are you going?"

"The name is Roseway! And I'm trying to find my way home. I'm just not sure where that is. All I have is this picture with an address on the back. I think it says 572......I can't read the name."

"Well, let me see it. What, you can't read? It says 572 King Street. That could be anywhere. When we get to the next city, we will look for some information at the library. However, that won't be for a couple of days. We really are way out in the boondocks. I bet you're hungry. Here, have a sandwich." Joseph reached into a cooler beside him and pulled out a sandwich.

Roseway grabbed the sandwich and took a little bite, and then a bigger one, until her mouth was full.

"Wow, slow down a little, you'll choke yourself eating too fast," Joseph said, as he passed her a pop from the cooler and smiled gently.

"Mmm, this is good," she said as she burped loudly. Roseway's serious facial expression lightened. She sat quietly for a while and then drifted off to sleep. Joseph placed a blanket on her slender body. He glanced at her often, pitying her unhealthy appearance. Her clothes were worn and dirty, and her hygiene was poor.

Joseph pulled into a truck stop for the night. He nudged Roseway to wake her up. She stretched, and for a moment forgot where she was. "What? Where are we?" she asked, wiping the sleep from her eyes.

"Here are some clean clothes, soap and shampoo. They belong to Gabrielle. You might as well use them. She left her bag in the back of the truck cab. There are showers where you can go wash yourself." He pointed to the restrooms.

Roseway stepped down from the big truck and went into the restroom and stripped off her dirty rags. She had never seen a shower like this. Roseway was used to bathing in the cold river not far from the cabin. She stood bewildered under the showerhead. *What am I supposed to do to make the water come out?* She looked at the taps on the wall and placed her hand on the red one. Instinctively, she tried to move it by shaking and pulling on it. Surprisingly, the tap turned and water started coming out of the showerhead above her. She then turned the other tap a twist. The water poured more strongly out of the showerhead onto her body. First it was cold and it chilled to the bone. Roseway turned the tap more. Then the water began to change temperature. Seconds later, she screamed as hot water came pouring over her. Hearing the scream, Joseph rushed in. Roseway tried to cover her nakedness. Joseph could see the hot steam coming from the shower. He turned the knob until the water was lukewarm.

"Are you all right? You didn't burn yourself did you?" He asked, trying not to look at her beautifully shaped body.

"I'm fine," she replied, trying to hide her embarrassment and the pain.

Joseph backed out of the restroom as Roseway continued to shower. Joseph's flushed face returned to its normal olive tone. His palms were sweaty. "Oh Lord, give me strength," he said under his breath.

When Roseway was done, she came out looking like a new penny. Joseph marvelled at the metamorphosis and found himself quite attracted to her. She was breathtakingly beautiful. Something seemed amiss to Joseph. *Why couldn't she read? Why did she not know how to use a shower? She looks like a woman, but seems immature in other ways. That is strange.* Joseph put his arm on her shoulder and suggested they get some food to eat.

They had burgers and some fries. The mustard and relish dripped off the burger and down her chin with each bite. She licked the sauce with her tongue as she moaned in delight, thoroughly enjoying the delicious taste. Roseway couldn't remember such a taste sensation. When she lived in the cabin, they never had the luxury of garnishes like mustard, relish, ketchup or salt and pepper. When she had finished eating, she wiped her mouth with the cuff of her sleeve.

Joseph threw her a napkin. "These are called napkins, and they are for wiping your face."

"Oh," Roseway replied as she raised her eyebrow in acknowledgment.

They rested in the truck cab for a few hours so Joseph could get some sleep. Roseway watched him. His head leaned against the window. He looked so peaceful and strong. Roseway felt such gratitude at how nicely he had treated her, thinking she must be dreaming. She couldn't understand these feelings she felt being around him—an attraction she had not felt before. It was like all the walls were coming down around her.

The sun was starting to rise in the early morning. Joseph ran into the truck stop diner and brought out a couple of egg sandwiches and coffees. "Well, off we go. We should make it to Prince George some time tonight." They pulled onto the road.

Roseway took a sip of her coffee and spit it out. "Yuck, what is this stuff? It tastes so bitter."

In disbelief Joseph laughed as he responded, "You have got to be kidding me, right? Haven't you tasted coffee before?"

Crinkling her nose, Roseway assured Joseph. "No, we never had coffee at the cabin or whatever you call this horrible tasting mud. Do you have any water?"

Joseph tossed a bottle of water to her and then continued to drive mile after mile. It was about midday and a hot thirty degrees Celsius in the cab of the truck. The air conditioning was not working.

Joseph knew of a nice waterfall just a few hours from Prince George. He thought it would be a lot of fun to stop and freshen up. Out of the truck, they proceeded to walk down the long path. As they neared the bottom of the hill, they could hear the cascading water hitting the rocks below. Joseph pulled off his shirt and pants, and then ran down to the water in his boxers. Like a young boy, enthusiastic and full of vibrant joy, he rushed into the water. His smile lit up his face and his eyes glistened like diamonds. Roseway watched his excitement and felt the spiritual awe of the moment. With such release, unafraid, she instinctively pulled off all her clothing and ran into the waterfall to join him. Joseph's mouth dropped as he looked at her naked body. They both found themselves enveloped in the awesome moment. Water gushed through the rocky crevices, creating a tranquil mist. Water fell fresh over their bodies like a cleansing rain. They laughed and splashed the water up with their hands.

For minutes, they stood under the falling water just looking up into the rainbow, soaking up the moment like a sponge. Then they looked at each other as the glow on their faces stared back. Their eyes seemed to look into each other's souls. Joseph extended his hand to Roseway, and she gently allowed her hand to fall into his like a flower into a vase. He walked her back to their clothing and he helped her put her top back on. Innocently, he noticed the beauty of her pear-shaped breasts. Then she picked up his shirt and pulled it up over his head and down over his muscular body. They hugged for a brief moment and simultaneously said, "That was awesome."

Together, they walked back to the truck hand in hand, singing silent praises to God while savouring the awe of the experience.

Back on the road, their conversation was pleasant. They talked about the scenery, the mountains. Joseph told some boyhood stories of camping with his friends. He was quite the outdoorsman. Canoeing was one of his favourite pastimes. He was also a bit of a thrill-seeker. There was not much he hadn't experienced at one time or another—everything from skydiving to mountain climbing and dirt bike racing.

Roseway slowly began to relax and open up herself to Joseph little by little. Her abdomen felt like it had little butterflies dancing within. Like a magnet pulling them together, she was finding herself more and more drawn to him.

Joseph, too, began to feel more and more intrigued as they talked. He prodded the conversation to go a little deeper. "Can you remember anything about your home?"

Roseway drifted off into a hypnotic gaze and stared out the truck window. The trees quickly rushed by, taking her back to a memory of years ago. In a quiet, reflective voice, Roseway began to tell Joseph what she remembered.

"My mom was hanging white bedding from the clothes line. I can still smell the freshness in the air. I can hear the sound of children's laughter. We had an old rusty swing set. It was orange. My brother and sister and I would play for hours on that swing set. We would sing that song, *Found a Peanut*. The song didn't have an end, because we made up our own verses. In our yard we had apple trees. I can still smell the sweet fragrance from the apple blossoms. The crab-apple trees were in full bloom. Pink blossoms clustere together, looking like a giant bouquet of flowers dancing in the sunny breeze.

"In the backyard we had a big slide made of wood with black railings. We had to climb this tall ladder to get to the top of the slide. I remember my sister Suzie sitting at the top. She is a couple years older than me. Her eyes are brown and she has curly blond hair. Anyway, it was a sunny day; big fluffy white cotton balls filled the sky. I was playing on the swing, while my brother Billy pushed me higher and higher. We were having so much fun that day.

"Then Mom hollered with her cheerful voice from the front porch, the way she always did. 'Come on in kids, lunch is ready.' Like a stampede, Billy and Suzie raced to the house. I waited for the swing to slow down a little. When it did, I tried to jump off even though the swing was still moving. In the process, my dress caught on the chain and it ripped. It made me fall to the ground and I scraped my knees.

"While I was lying on the ground, a tall dark shadow blocked out the sun—a shadow that would be over me for years to come. His name was Joe. I called him Big Joe or BJ. He was a familiar man from around town. At that moment, he seemed friendly as he bent down to take a look at my knee. He wiped the tear from my eye.

With his Newfoundlander accent, he said, 'Let me help ya. I ave a bandage in my car.'"

"Gently he took me by the hand and I trustingly went with him. I never thought anything of it. I just thought we were going to get a bandage. Pointing to the back seat, he said, 'Sit ere and I'll get da bandage.'

"When I sat down, he quickly pushed my legs into the car and closed the door. He ran around the car to the driver's seat, locked the doors and sped off. Still, I remember so clearly, pulling on the door handle of the car. I was screaming and crying, 'Let me out! I want to go home.' I watched from the back seat as we drove farther and farther away from my house. BJ stopped the car for only a second. He ran to the side door and opened it and reached in and grabbed my arm. Big Joe whaled me in the side of the head. The blow left a stinging red handprint on my face. My ears rang from the blow. He yelled, 'Shut up! Stop your cryin.'

"The trees went by the window. I was so afraid—afraid to cry or make a peep. Yet I couldn't hold back the sobs as I cried myself to sleep.

"The rest is a blur, until waking up in that ole log cabin where he and I lived for the last twelve years. I think that is how long it has been since I was taken from my home. I'm not even sure how old I am now. I think I was about six years old when he took me from my home. Many times I tried to run away from him. There was really nowhere for me to run. BJ would always find me. He'd give me such a beating. He'd say, 'If you run away like dat again, I'll go back ta dat ole ouse of yours. I'll kill your Momma, liddle Suzie and Billy too. Do ya want dat ta appen, ah?' He always put the living fear into me."

As Roseway recounted her memories, tears flowed endlessly down her face and neck. Joseph passed her a clean hankie, to wipe away the tears.

Joseph asked, "Where was your dad when all this happened?"

"I don't know much about my dad. Momma never talked about him. She said he died around the time I was born. When I did ask about my dad, Momma would say, 'Never mind about him.' I guess Uncle Jim was the closest thing we had to a Dad. He'd be at our house from time to time." Roseway continued to cry as she told her story.

Joseph could see the topic was overwhelming her. With the loud sound of the air breaks, he pulled his rig over to the side of the road. His eyes watered and he kept trying to swallow the lump in his throat, trying not to cry too. He wanted to console Roseway in her emotional breakdown. The truck came to a stop and Joseph reached over to give Roseway a hug. She sobbed on his shoulder with such release. "That is okay, Roseway; just cry and let go of all that hurt and pain. It is okay to cry. Everything will be alright now. You will see."

Joseph rubbed his strong but gentle hand over her soft, mahogany hair. He rubbed her back. Roseway had never experienced this kind of touch. As she melted into his arms—it felt so good to be touched in a loving manner. His hug was intoxicating and pacifying. For a moment she felt warmth seep deep into her bones. She could feel some of her pain expel as her sobs subdued. Joseph put his head close to hers. He had such a compassionate feeling in his heart. "It will be okay, Roseway." He spoke softly.

The closeness of her body melting into his was soothing. Their emotions began to flow deep into the embrace. The earthy smell of her hair tantalized his senses. Her skin felt soft like silk on his stubbly face. Instinctively, Joseph began to kiss away her tears. His gentle lips felt soft and warm on her cheeks. Heat ran through her veins with each kiss. She tilted her head until their lips met like two converging butterflies. A drug of passion made the hairs on her arm stand up straight. Both felt a passionate desire develop through the kiss. Roseway felt an overpowering desire of want and need flow to the pit of her stomach. She couldn't understand these feelings, but knew she wanted more. It felt so good—so right. Joseph felt it, too. He had kissed other girls before, but none had left him with such a chemical explosion that even made his legs go weak. His strong convictions told him it was going too fast. He felt the lack of control taking over his rational thinking. *This feels so good. I want to continue. Everything in me says more, but God I know this is wrong. It is too soon, but just a little longer. No, I've got to stop this now or soon I won't be able to control my passion. Who do I please? Do I do what is right in your eyes, God, or follow my desires?* Abruptly, Joseph pulled away.

"We can't do this, Roseway." Roseway was confused how something that felt so right could be so wrong. She tried to pull him back to continue the kiss. Joseph put his hands on her shoulders to separate their bodies. Joseph panted in frustration, "No!"

The sternness in his voice sent throngs of pain into her stomach. Her face flushed, feeling hurt and confusion. This ignited a defensive anger from the rejection she felt. *I don't understand? Why is he stopping? What did I do wrong? Why is he angry with me? Is he punishing me like Big Joe?* These feelings churned in her stomach and built up like a volcano ready to erupt. She reacted with a negative response to Joseph and began to pull away from him. His emotions tugged hard between his heart and mind and he froze, not knowing what to say or do next.

With a fleeing instinct, Roseway pushed him back and said defensively, "Fine then." Flailing like a drowning child, she accidentally hit Joseph in the face. All her uncontrolled emotions began to well up within her again as she yelled irrational words at him. Her voice sounded wrought with dejection as she screeched aloud, crying, working herself into an unreasonable state of mind.

Roseway grabbed the bag on the seat, opened the truck door and bolted out. With all her might she raced away from the truck and headed toward the bush. Somehow she felt if she ran far from the pain of the rejection she was feeling, it would go away. Her illogical thoughts and feelings always seemed to pull her like a magnet, running back to that place of seclusion—to that place where she always tried to find a tiny morsel of something familiar, something she could trust. In this place of desperation, she always found herself face to face with humility, causing her to seek God's help in this place where she would hear His voice and find His hope.

Joseph raced out of the truck and ran after her. He tripped over a rock and banged his knee. As he hobbled to his feet, he yelled, "Roseway, come on back. Come back! I didn't mean to......I just wanted to help......you. We are not too far from Prince George, maybe a couple of hours. We will see what we can do to get you home. Roseway, come back!" Roseway was out of sight and running away so determinedly that she never heard his call.

Frustrated at the outcome, Joseph kicked the dirt. "Oh God, what did I do?" Angry with himself, he punched the truck door. Joseph leaned against the truck and slid down to the ground like a wounded soldier. He felt the blow and was down for the count.

"Well, that is just great, God. I tried to do the right thing in your eyes and look what happened. I'm here and she is gone. I'll never find her out here in the middle of the mountains and trees. What should I do now?" Joseph sat and continued to pray.

He slept in the truck all night, hoping she would return. Morning came and there was still no sign of her to be found. Joseph started up the truck and drove toward Prince George.

3
ICON

Roseway kept running, never looking back. Still crying from the hurt she felt, she entered into a wooded area. Roseway ran until she could hardly breathe. Her heart was pounding like tribal drums. After running aimlessly for a couple of miles, she stopped to rest. It was nearing nightfall, and Roseway was too exhausted to make a shelter. She found a little place of refuge in amongst some rocks. Curled up in a little ball to keep warm, she settled down for the night.

Emotionally drained, Roseway began to talk with God. God was the only person she could talk to for so many years. It came so naturally to her. With her vivid imagination, she could allow her mind to open up to God. His voice to her was like a voice in the desert. As a young child, Roseway had developed a special relationship with her Saviour. Through the Holy Spirit, she was given the ability to hear God's voice. By the Spirit she learned many spiritual truths. It was the conversations they shared which held her together and made her strong. In her mind, God became both her mother and father. That was the only way she could cope with living with Big Joe. Though she didn't always get the answers she wanted from the Lord, He always directed her path. Here she was once again seeking His face like she did every day in that meadow.

Lord, it is a full moon tonight but the dark clouds backwash over the moon and stars. The sky is a dispiriting funnel of death. Are those water droplets falling from the sky your tears? They can't be. You seem so far away. Then again, perhaps you are crying with me today? That would give my heart some comfort. My heart cries a river of tears. I'm so tired. I don't know what to do or where to go from here. It feels like a thousand years of hurt and disappointment are bottled up within me. I'm so weary, lonely and sad—an ugly sore, festering with poison, a pimple ready to explode—trapped in a bubble of pity and confusion, like a fly in a spider's web. I'm overwhelmed with uncertainty. Still, I am smart enough to know, I do need you Lord. Without you I have nothing.

At this point, she could hear God's still, quiet voice whisper within her spirit. She lifted her head toward heaven and listened to His voice.

ROSEWAY, YOU MUST REACH DOWN TO THE DEEPEST PART OF YOUR FAITH, TO WHERE MY SPIRIT PATIENTLY WAITS. EVEN IN THE DARKEST PLACES, YOU CAN FIND THE LIGHT OF MY STRENGTH. YOU MUST CONQUER YOUR FEAR. YOU ARE MY CHILD AND I UNDERSTAND YOUR FEAR. BE STRONG AND COURAGEOUS. GO AND LOOK INTO THE DARKNESS, AND FACE THE MONSTERS OF YOUR PAST, WHICH ARE HIDDEN WITHIN THAT EXPECTANT FEAR. PERFECT LOVE CASTS OUT ALL FEAR. TRUST IN ME, THE LORD YOUR GOD. YOUR FAITH WILL HELP YOU OVERCOME YOUR FEARS AND YOUR DISAPPOINTMENTS. I WILL BE THE LIGHT IN YOUR DARKNESS. BE READY TO FACE THE UNEXPECTED REALITY TO BE REVEALED IN YOU. FOR WHEN YOU LOOK, YOU WILL BE ABLE TO SEE ALL THAT HINDERS YOU AND OVERCOME THESE OBSTACLES. AT SUCH A YOUNG AGE, THE POWERS OF DARKNESS BEGAN TO DESTROY A HEART OF INNOCENCE. THUS THE DUNGEON GATE WAS OPENED

AND THEN CLOSED AS A WAY OF SELF-PROTECTION. NOW IT IS TIME TO LOOK IN THAT DARK DUNGEON AND FACE THE RAGING SIDE OF YOURSELF. FOR IN THAT DARKNESS THE HEALING LIGHT OF CHRIST CAN RESTORE THE YEARS WHICH WERE STOLEN, AND HEAL THE SCARS FROM DEEP WITHIN YOUR WOUNDED SOUL. I AM WITH YOU ALWAYS, WHEREVER YOU MAY GO. I ENCOURAGE YOU TO FACE THE DEFLOWERED, LAME, FRIGHTENED LITTLE CHILD WHO HAS BEEN LOCKED AWAY FOR SUCH A LONG TIME. SHE IS A PART OF YOU. ROSEWAY, YOU HAVE THE ABILITY TO UNLOCK THAT DUNGEON. SEEK WISDOM AND UNDERSTANDING. I WILL DIRECT YOUR PATH. HOLD ON TO YOUR FAITH.

Yes Lord! I recognize that little child who was held captive in such darkness, a child full of fear, hurt, and pain. That child is me. I'm afraid of the sounds around me, afraid of the unknown. Help me Lord to find my way in these dark places.

Roseway began to sing a song.

I cry Abba, I cry Daddy, I cry out.
Hold your little baby with your love, with your love.
Remove the fowler's snare, the coiling web of fear.
Complete in me your perfect love.
Feed the hunger deep within, so I no longer sin.
Let me feel you, while I am still.
I pray you set me free from the chains that surround me,
Chains which keep me from loving you.
Do a work within my heart. Your love to me impart,
In the fullness, of your perfect love.

Roseway sang until she drifted off into a deep sleep.

The night was a black spade of darkness. The deck of cards fell to the ground. Roseway was walking down a long muddy path. Mud was sticking to her worn-out shoes. She pushed branches away as they hit her face. The trees had grimacing faces. They chanted as she walked. "Roseway, Roseway, you can't run away from me. You are mine, Roseway. You're a bad girl. I'll punish you, Roseway." The voices haunted her, tugging at her mind. She clasped her hands over her ears as she walked.

A foggy mist lay near to the ground. Eerie sounds were all around. Something rustled in the bush beside her. Roseway quickened her pace. The faster she walked, the louder the sounds. She slipped and slid in the mud. Growls pierced the darkness, not just one but many. Their eyes gazed through the trees as the clouds moved swiftly across the moon, owls hooting, branches snapping.

Suddenly, Roseway lost her footing and began to slide down an embankment. Tree roots reached out from both sides as if waiting to catch and strangle her. Falling, falling, falling, Roseway bounced from one side of the steep grade to the other until she landed at the bottom in a miry pit of thick mud. It seemed to pull at her like a thousand arms. When she stood up from her fallen position, she looked upward. Wolves surrounded the pit on every side, waiting to devour her. Fear gripped her mind. She felt numb and helpless, trapped in the muddy pit. Feeling exhausted, her arms flailed to escape the pit.

Pulling her legs through the miry clay, she felt the bite of razor-like teeth break through her flesh, crushing the bone in her arm. She screamed another tormented scream, feeling like hell had her in its grip. With excruciating pain, she tried to pull her arm free from the iron jaws of the growling wolf. He was the leader of the pack. His eyes were black, though fire sparkled in his pupils.

He was dark grey and bigger than the other wolves, which seemed to be awaiting his command to attack. They growled ferociously.

Suddenly a white wolf appeared, teeth bared in a growl to show his superiority. His ears stood straight like sharp knives and his tail was long, drawn like a sword from its sheath. The white wolf began to defeat all the other wolves. He sprang from one wolf to the other like a flying gazelle. One after the other fell to the ground motionless, until they were all down except the big grey wolf. The white wolf howled victoriously. The fur on the back of his neck stood straight. Roseway felt a release of her arm. The grey wolf cowered and slowly turned to face its foe. They danced around each other like old-time rivals, giving each other death stares. With an eerie sound, the two collided, biting at each other's necks. Who would draw first blood? They rolled around the pit, over the other wolves' lifeless bodies. Blood sprayed like rain. One final cry invaded the air and then there was silence.

Roseway sat in shock, holding her bloody arm close to her chest. Her heart still pounded. The white wolf came over to Roseway. Their eyes met in the darkness of the night. Roseway was too overcome and too exhausted to fear or flinch. Then Roseway felt his sharp teeth bite into the back of her pants. He pulled her from the muddy pit. He licked her wounds and the scratches on her face.

Roseway jolted, awakened from her nightmare, holding her pounding chest and feeling her arm. Sweat beaded her brow as she took a breath of relief. "It was a dream."

The sun's warmth started shining through the trees. A startling noise rustled in the trees behind her. She gasped and slowly turned around to look at what was making the noise. There he stood, quietly whimpering, a white shepherd dog about a year old. His paw was caught in a crevice between two rocks. He was alone, afraid, helpless and in need of someone to care for him. His eyes were a soft brown, sunken behind his long nose. His coat was thick and had a healthy sheen. Big ears stood straight up and so did his long white tail. Roseway gently released his bruised paw and kissed it better. She hugged him with her arms like a mother with a child. "Where did you come from, little fellow?"

The young dog tickled her face with kisses, making her laugh. "I think I'll call you Whitey, or how about Icon? Yeah, I'll name you Icon. You were in my dream. You're my little gift from God. Aren't you, Icon? I like that name. Thank you, Lord."

5
A TIME TO BE STILL

There was a new day on the horizon and Roseway and Icon had another path to follow. Roseway had a new loyal companion, a friend to break the loneliness. He walked by her side with every step she took. They traipsed deeper into the forest of evergreen and coniferous trees. Embedded amongst the rocky terrain were hardwood trees such as Birch and Poplar, softwood trees like Red Cedar and tall pine trees with trunks spanning five feet in diameter.

Roseway looked for a place to build a permanent shelter that would get her through the fall and winter. She could tell fall was on its way by the shorter days and cool nights. Not far from a river she found a good place to set up a little camp. At times she would trip over Icon while working diligently. He wanted to help, too.

When camp was set up, they could play. Roseway looked for a good throwing stick for Icon to fetch. She found a nice straight branch and threw it into the river. "Fetch, Icon," she commanded.

With ears pointed straight up, he ran, jumped into the water and brought her back the stick. Roseway looked at the stick and had an idea to make a bow and arrow. During the twelve years Roseway lived back at the old cabin with Big Joe, she went hunting with him many times and she became quite the marksman. Despite her feminine exterior, Roseway had a tough tomboy side to her, which had developed from being treated roughly by BJ. He was a no-nonsense man who taught her many things about survival in the outdoors. Roseway was always told when she didn't do something the right way, which really meant it wasn't done BJ's way. Etched in Roseway's memory was the first time she held a bow. Her mind slipped back to a time when she and BJ walked slowly through the forest. With intense quiet, they could hear the breeze whistle through the trees.

"Shhh, look over there," he whispered.

There was a big jackrabbit sitting eating leaves, ears erect. Its little nose wiggled as it chewed. Its little eyes froze as it sat still.

"Roseway." BJ elbowed her. "Pull your bow back, aim and let the arrow go." Roseway could feel her eyes water. She felt the battle inside of her. Looking eye to eye with the rabbit, she shook her head, not wanting to kill it.

"Big Joe, I can't." BJ nudged her shoulder roughly, getting impatient. Agitated, he pulled back his bow. You could hear the arrow cut through the air and the crack as it pierced the rabbit, which fell over dead. BJ yanked back Roseway's head as he grabbed her hair with his big hand.

Angrily he snapped at her. "Next time, ya shoot da dam ting when I tell ya to. Now get your ass over dare and get dat rabbit. Ya can carry it back to da cabin. Wipe dat stuff out of your eyes too." Then he slapped her in the back of the head, pushing her toward the rabbit. "Pick it up and let's go."

Roseway snapped her thoughts back to her present task at hand. The thoughts in her head turned like a wheel, thinking of what she would need. First she would need something sharp. Roseway plunged into the river and started picking up stones, looking to find a sharp one to use for a knife. While reaching into the water, she cut her finger on the razor-sharp edge of a stone. Once she had her sharp stone, she proceeded to look for a strong branch to make a bow. She found a thick branch from a fir tree, strong yet bendable. Finding just the right size of branch, she whittled away with the stone and cut both ends of the shaft of the stick. When the ends of the stick were slightly pointed, she cut a deep ridge about an inch from both ends. The shaft of the bow was about two feet long. With the sharp stone, she cut long strips of cloth from her old blue jeans, and then began to braid the threads tightly together. She then tied the braided string tight to the shaft, completing the bow.

She found straight poplar branches about two feet long. The wood was strong and good for whittling arrows. There must have been a forest fire some years back. These are the kinds of trees that grow amongst the Spruce Forests of British Columbia.

With the stone, Roseway carved and scraped the branches down until they were long, smooth, pointed arrows. After finding feathers from the remains of a dead half-eaten grouse, she used pinesap to affix the bird feathers to the arrows. Icon was in a playful mood, and took one of the arrows. He started to run away with the arrow, teasing Roseway, running in circles as if to say, "Come and get it from me."

Not in the mood for playing, Roseway called, "Hey, get back here with that. Come, Icon. Drop it." Roseway chased him and surrendered to play his little game of chase. She grabbed the stick and they played tug of war. Then she took it from him. "Look what you did, Icon. You put teeth marks all over it. It's not much good, now. That was going to get us some meat for supper. Here, I'll try shooting it anyway and see how my bow works."

Roseway put the arrow in her bow and pulled gently on the braided string to work the bow and stretch it a little. Then she pulled it back and let it go. "Icon, fetch." Eagerly, Icon ran after it.

But he didn't come back right away. "Icon, come here boy!" For a moment a bit of fear rose up in Roseway's stomach. She ran to see where he went.

Down the river from their camp, hidden amongst the forest, was a log cabin. There was Icon sniffing around trying to find the arrow. Roseway kicked up her heels in excitement. She could hardly believe what she saw. "Yahoo, will you look at that!"

She ran up to the door, which was ajar. There was no one to be found anywhere near the cabin. It looked like it had been abandoned some time ago. The cabin was made of mostly pine logs, packed well with clay, stones and grass. There were no windows, just a small smoke stack on the roof. The door had big claw marks running down it, as if a bear had been to visit and tried to get into the cabin, possibly looking for food. Outside the cabin was a pile of wood that had been stacked but knocked over. There was an axe hanging on the wall. Roseway would have to get more wood to get her through the winter.

Inside the cabin in one corner was a little wood stove with a pan on top. Against the wall were a couple of homemade bunks with some dusty blankets. The cabin looked rundown and would need a little work to make it winter-worthy. There was a box of matches sitting on top of the stove beside an old lantern full of oil. She picked up the box and shook it. "Thank you, Lord." She whispered. There was not much more to find that was of any good use, as she rummaged through the few cupboards on the wall. There was a box of empty glass jars she could use for preserving fruit. The cabin was pretty much cleared out by whoever had stayed there before. On a homemade table sat a water basin with a few eating utensils—a plate, cups, forks and knives. The table and a couple of chairs were carved from the trunk of an ash tree. There were a few old newspapers and an old worn bible on the table.

"Maybe I could use these to light the stove? Hmm," she sighed, as she opened up the bible and blew the dust from its pages. It opened up to Psalm 23.

Roseway could only read at a grade one level. Her eyes fell to the page. She tried to pronounce the words. "The... Lo-rd is my shep-herd; I will la-ck no-thing. Her eyes brightened remembering that prayer she had said for many years when she went to talk with the Lord at her meadow of loneliness. Roseway continued to read, but Icon playfully bit at her pant leg. She put down the bible, bent, and petted his head and said, "Good boy, Icon." She couldn't stop smiling. "Well Icon, come on. Let's get us some food."

Roseway filled her days by piling wood and collecting many of the different kinds of berries which grow in the British Columbia forests. Big Joe had taught Roseway a lot of the knowledge he had learned from the aboriginals. Buffalo berries, or soapberries, are deciduous shrubs with small, reddish orange fruits. She knew how to crush soapberries with water to make her favourite concoction.

Chokecherries are red or black. They grow in long clusters. They have large stones and can be somewhat sour to taste, but are good for making jellies, juices and syrups. Also the high bush cranberries are tall shrubs with tart, clustered fruits, which are good in sauces and desserts. Blackberries, blueberries, bilberries, and huckleberries are also edible fruits she would preserve. There are more than two hundred species of wild fruits in British Columbia's interior. Some are poisonous, some edible and others unpalatable. No rules exist for telling them apart. Roseway was taught at a young age which ones she could eat. They grow at different times throughout the seasons.

Fiddleheads and wild mushrooms were also a mainstay in her diet until the snow arrived. She hunted rabbit, deer and any animal that moved. Grouse was her easiest prey to catch. They were not easily frightened.

Change was quickly making its appearance as the days became shorter and shorter. There was crispness in the changing of the season. Hidden in the quiet of each moment was a vibrant hope as the leaves on the trees seemed to come alive with colour. The night air was cool and fresh. Each evening, dew blanketed the ground like a heavenly breath.

The days came and went. Roseway collected different leaves, Rose Hips, Hemlock and Spruce needles for a good source of vitamin C. She boiled them in water and drank it like tea. With the rabbit and deer furs, she made herself a warm winter coat, sewing her furs together using the tendons of the animals. With the antlers she made a spear. Roseway looked for anything she could find—things left behind from previous visitors. She found some aluminum cans and some wire, useful for trapping. Up in one of the trees close to the cabin was a bird trap.

Roseway made her own soap. She collected wood branches and burned them. Next, she poured water over the ashes and gathered up the by-product of water from the ashes, called lye water. She would mix the lye water with animal fat and cook it over a fire, stirring slowly until the fat melted and blended with the water. She made a mould out the clay from the bank of the river. When they had hardened, she poured the soap into the mould. When it hardened, she cut it into small bars of soap, which she used for washing.

Each day, Roseway worked herself to exhaustion, knowing winter would be upon them soon. Icon became quite the skilled hunter himself, sniffing down the scent of animals. Sometimes, when Roseway only wounded their prey, Icon made the final kill by shaking the animal by the scruff of the neck. By winter, Icon had grown to his full size.

At the end of each gruelling day, they both settled in the cabin for the night. Roseway would light a fire in the stove and cook some food. It became part of the routine to open the old black book and guess at some of the words, to read a bible verse. An orange glow from the pipes softly illuminated the cabin walls. She would pet Icon's fur as he nuzzled his head close beside her. They were constant companions. Many nights, they would both fall asleep on the floor by the fire. The only visitors they had were the mice that ran across the rafters.

The October winds chilled. Roseway built a very small underground freezer. There she would store some of her meat and preserves in the frozen ground. The colder days and nights enabled the meat to last longer for their winter food supply.

Snow began to fall each day, making the days seem ever so long. When the snow came it gave the crude freezer an extra covering of insulation, which helped defeat some of the odours that could attract other animals. It became more difficult to go far from the cabin or hunt as the snow deepened. With a good food supply, though, they could stay in the cabin for days on end. When they did, Roseway found comfort doing a little sewing or scraping the furs and playing with Icon.

Many days, snowflakes the size of cotton balls fell from the sky, covering the ground like a blanket of white. The snow was too deep to walk any long distance. Using some of the skin from the furs, Roseway put together some makeshift snowshoes, so she wouldn't sink into the snow. She never went too far from the cabin, only venturing out when it was time to check some of the traps she had set. The amazing sight of God's hand-painted landscape gave her a sense of serenity and she felt God's presence ever so near. The snow crested the trees.

When the snow stopped and the sun came out, Roseway and Icon both ventured outdoors. The trees looked like giant white statues. The snow statues stood out vividly in front of the blue sky, sparkling like diamonds from the sun's rays. Roseway paused and took a breath of the air, embracing the beauty surrounding her. In the stillness she talked to God and felt his presence.

Lord, here I sit under the warmth of the sun being warmed to the depth of my soul. I feel the essence of serenity. Even the coldness of winter's wind cannot quench the sunny rays. No chill in my bones. Sunlight brings nourishment for another day. There is a hope for tomorrow. Thank you, Lord.

A genuine smile complemented the softness of her rosy cheeks. Roseway made snow angels under the clear blue sky while Icon bounced through the snow playfully, lifting the snow with his nose. She laughed at him, watching him barrel roll through the snow upside down. He washed his fur on the snow, looking like an old polar bear caked in white. Roseway threw snowballs at him. Icon bit through them as he caught them and ate the snow. The two became ever so close as winter dragged on one month at a time.

Eventually, the days started to get longer. Spring would bring some mild days melting the snow. The rivers opened up. Bow and arrows in hand, Roseway and Icon went out each spring day to check the traps and hunt up some food. By the time spring arrived, their winter supplies were getting low. The ground was thronged with mud from the melted snow. Buds on the trees looked like candy sprouting from the branch stems. The trees waited patiently for the warmth of the sun to clothe their naked branches with the fullness of bright green leaves. The wind was howling in circles. Like violently shaken children, the tree branches tossed back and forth. Rooted deeply into the ground, the trees stood firm against the strain, never hanging their heads in defeat.

One day, when Roseway and Icon arrived back at the cabin, the door was pushed from its hinges. Icon started barking, acting crazy. He paced back and forth near the underground food shelter. He growled and barked. A grizzly bear walk out from behind the shelter and stood on his hind legs. A roar belted from the deep.

Roseway yelled, "Icon, here boy!" The bear stood its ground. The fur on Icon's neck stood tall. Roseway shot an arrow into the bear's shoulder. It didn't slow the bear down. It turned and started to run toward her. Roseway loaded her bow again and let another arrow fly, hitting the bear a second time. The bear still kept running toward her. Icon lunged at the quickly moving bear, sinking his teeth into the bear's paw. Roseway yelled at the top of her lungs, "Icon, no!" She ran and grabbed the axe from the cabin wall. The bear growled fiercely. When Roseway heard Icon yelp, she turned around quickly. The bear bit down on Icon's neck, then shook him. With his other paw the bear knocked Icon from his grip.

With adrenaline and fear, Roseway flung the axe at the bear, hitting it in the head. The bear fell to the ground stunned. Roseway picked the axe up off the ground then proceeded to hit the bear over the head until she was sure it was dead. She turned around to talk to Icon. "We got him, didn't we boy?"

In disbelief, Roseway stopped in her tracks. Her eyes grew big upon her paling face. She looked at Icon lying so still before her. His eyes darkened with a blank glaze.

"Icon. . ." She cried. Standing over the fallen dog, she felt afraid to touch him. Sporadic breaths wheezed from his nostrils as his lungs filled with a breath. Paralyzed with fear, Icon didn't know what had hit him. He cried with a helpless whine. Roseway patted his stomach, trying to hold in her tears, not knowing what to do. She felt helpless and so alone. "Oh God, what do I do?" All she could think to do was to keep running her hand along his long, soft-coated body. He tried to raise his head, whining to her like a child to a mother. Then his tongue hung limp from his mouth as his head fell back down and his stomach stopped moving.

Icon's body lay so still. Roseway's eyes watered, feeling the break of their bond cut in two. He was dead. It felt like her heart was ripped from her chest and her world came crashing down. She lifted him in her arms as she began to sob uncontrollably. Tears flowed from her eyes. Her eyes stung with sorrow. You could hear her scream echo through the forest. "No!" She wailed like a wild animal until her throat hurt.

The next day, Roseway dug a deep grave using the axe and her bare hands. She lifted Icon's heavy body down into the hole in the ground. Hesitantly, she kicked the dirt over him, holding in her tears as long as she could. On a little grave marker made out of wood, she carved his name. It was a time to be still. For days, Roseway sat in silence. She lay on her bunk and stared at the ceiling. Nothing seemed to matter anymore. Her eyes were puffy from crying. She felt such despairing loneliness. Every so often, her emotions welled up from within her and she cried and cried out to God. "Why? Why?"

A still quiet voice seemed to whisper, IT'S TIME TO MOVE ON, ROSEWAY. FOR I KNOW THE PLANS I HAVE FOR YOU, PLANS TO PROSPER YOU AND NOT TO HARM YOU, PLANS TO GIVE YOU HOPE AND A FUTURE.

"I can't do this. I don't know how. I don't know anything. Where will I stay? What will I eat? Where do I begin to start?"

6
TEST OF FAITH

Gathering up the few belongings she owned, Roseway stuffed her bag. She stopped for one final goodbye at Icon's grave. "I really loved you. I miss you so much. Thanks for being my friend. I'll never have another friend like you. Bye, Icon." She picked a spring flower and placed it on his grave. Wiping the tear from her eye, she turned and solemnly walked away.

Roseway walked in the direction of the sun all day until she came to a road. The sun began to set and darkness covered the landscape. In the distance she could see an amazing spectacle of light brighten the sky. The sign on the roadside read: "Welcome to Prince George." Roseway walked the road well into the night. Big trucks and fast cars raced by her, reminding her of Joseph. She wondered if she would ever see him again.

* * *

When Roseway ran off, Joseph had driven into Prince George and went to the police station to enquire about a missing child from twelve years ago.

He found out that there was a missing child by the name of Rose Shaffer. A little six-year-old child kidnapped from her home in the small town of Kelowna, British Columbia. The police told Joseph to hang around while they did their search. Police said they would do a search of the bush area where Joseph last saw her. But their search came up empty. The police brought Joseph in and held him overnight for questioning the next day.

The case had been closed for a few years. Investigator John Keffer received the phone call from the police and reopened the case. He was the original agent heading the investigation when Rose Shaffer had first disappeared. Keffer was a hard case, high bent on finding her. He was coming up for a review and hoping for a promotion to staff sergeant of the Royal Canadian Mounted Police Missing Women Task Force. Nothing would look better on his resume than to solve this case. Keffer made the drive to Prince George.

Joseph waited in the interrogation room for what seemed like hours. The room was small, nine-feet square, almost claustrophobic with its grey cracked walls and only one mirror on the wall. It made him feel freaky, sitting in the hard uncomfortable chair, knowing that someone was probably watching him through the two-way mirror.

Keffer entered the room wearing a white dress shirt, black tie and pants. His face looked stern and his body posture was un-friendly as he walked around the table to stand across from Joseph. He rested his foot on a chair and leaned his elbow on his thigh, holding himself upright. Annoyingly, Keffer clicked his pen on and off. The noise seemed magnified in Joseph's ears—click, click, click. Joseph murmured under his breath, *"I can't believe this is happening. How did I get myself into this mess? I was only trying to help find Rose."*

"So Joseph, tell me about the girl you picked up recently. Your statement says that you picked her up out near Yellow Knife. How many days ago was that?"

"I guess it was about a week ago."

"What was it, a week ago, five days ago, or four? What exactly was it?"

"What difference does it make?"

"Just answer the questions. What are you doing picking up young girls, anyway?"

"Hey man, she looked lost. She was way out in the middle of nowhere. Initially I just stopped to see if she was all right. She looked like she just crawled out of a hole. As it turned out, she needed a ride. I'm telling you she didn't even know where she lived, where she came from or where she was going. I tried to help her."

"You also said in your statement that you and she had a fight and that she ran back into the forest. What did you fight about?"

"That doesn't matter. What matters is that she is out there in the forest somewhere and we need to find her."

"Just maybe you killed her and put her body somewhere?"

"That is just ridiculous! Why would I come into the police for help if I did that?"

"Maybe you are just trying to cover your tracks."

"Listen, are you charging me with a crime? I'm not going to say another word unless I have some legal representation present."

Joseph no sooner spoke the words when the door opened. A tall, plump man walked into the room.

"Hello Joseph, I'm Corporal Higgins, in charge of the detachment. We have done a background check on you. We have nothing to hold you on. However, don't leave the province within the next couple of days. We may need to question you again."

Joseph was frustrated with the search results and his own inability to do much to help Roseway. While he was being held in custody, he prayed fervently for her.

Lord, I feel like I should have run after her. In some way I feel I could have done more to help her. I blame myself for her running away. If I could help her, I would. I can't imagine her being lost out there all alone. I pray you protect her, Lord. Help her find her way home.

One night, Joseph had a dream. In that dream he could see Roseway sitting in a field of trees made of cement. It was dark. He could see many night shadows. In the darkness was a little church with a brightly lit cross above it. He could see her surrounded by a bubble of glass. She looked frightened. Roseway was pounding on the glass, trying to get out. Then Joseph saw the glass shatter and he awoke from his dream. He kept the dream in mind.

Joseph headed back to his home in Kamloops. He told his parents about the events which occurred on his trip home.

For months, Joseph tossed and turned each night, having that same dream again and again. His head beaded with sweat and he would awaken from his sleep. Joseph wondered why he kept having that dream. Over that winter, Joseph continued to work. Every time he passed a young woman on the street he thought of Rose. She was always on his mind. He prayed for her every day.

One morning, Joseph got up out of bed and talked to his parents. "I think maybe I'm supposed to go to Prince George again."

"Why? Do you think you might find her there, after all this time?" His mother asked, while pouring him a coffee.

"There is no explanation other than I feel drawn to go back there. I have a truckload to take in that direction anyway. Spring is here. I keep having that same dream. I was trying to think what significance that dream might have. Perhaps the field of cement trees represents a city. Prince George is the closest city from where

Roseway ran off. Maybe she found her way there. I don't know. I can't rest until I go there and look. Should I have stayed longer in Prince George when I was there last time?" The unrest Joseph felt was enough for him to head back to Prince George, drop off his truckload and have a look around.

* * *

The sun was rising. Roseway found herself walking into a busy metropolis of rush-hour traffic, people, and noise. Befuddled by this new world she found herself in, she looked around taking mental notes. The contrast from being in the bush to being in a city was magnified in the sound all around her. In disarray, she crossed the street. A car almost hit her, and then the driver honked his horn and yelled at her. "You stupid idiot, watch where you're going!" She ran out of the traffic, sat down and leaned up against a dumpster. With her knees tight to her chest, eyes closed and hands over her ears, Roseway tried to block out all the newfangled sounds.

Suddenly, Roseway heard the clanging of cans and a thrashing noise coming from inside the dumpster. Tin cans flew through the air—one can, then another, and then another, landing on the ground in front of her. Roseway turned her head and glanced up to look at who was climbing out of the dumpster. It was a young woman about nineteen. She had her blond hair in a ponytail. Her eyes were blue like the sky. Her pale complexion and soft features made her seem harmless. She jumped down from the dumpster, lost her balance, and found herself sprawled on the ground.

Initially, this young girl had no inclination of friendliness toward Roseway. When Roseway asked her who she was, the girl blurted, "This is my dumpster. So are the ones anywhere near here. You best move on from here."

Roseway sat confused at this girl's reaction. "What are you talking about? I don't want your dirty dumpster."

"What are you doing hanging around it?"

"I was just resting. I just arrived in town."

"If you know what's good for you, you will go back home now."

"I would go home, but I don't know where home is. Right now, home is where I lay my head. Besides, I don't recall asking for your advice."

"Well, I was just saying...I know what it's like around here."

"I don't really have much choice. I have nowhere to go."

"Most people in this town don't take kindly to another street bum. There are too many here already. A lot of homeless around here. Hey, it's everyone for them self around here. That's why I have claim to this dumpster. I recycle the cans and bottles, anything I can find so I can buy some food. Sometimes I work at the Cancun. It's a bit of a dive, but I make a little money on tips for doing a little dancing. Not enough to rent my own place, though. You might get the odd handout. Not too often in this town. Most people can't afford to give away money. The ones that do have money are too greedy to give spare change. I wouldn't take their handouts, anyway. I wouldn't want to give them the gratification to puff up their egos so they can feel better than me. Who wants their pity?"

"Well, I'm not a street bum. I have a home, and I'm going to find it."

"Are you stupid or something? What do you mean you can't find your home? How do you lose where you live? Do you have amnesia or something?"

"It's a long story. I don't want to talk about it."

"With your attitude, you're going get yourself in trouble."

"I don't have an attitude. You, however, are very rude."

"Oh, name calling now. I was going to say that I might be able to help you out a little. Who knows, maybe we could even become friends?"

Roseway mumbled, "I don't need anyone. Anyway, why would you want to be my friend?"

This odd girl persisted in the conversation. "I don't know. Maybe you remind me of myself? Or maybe I'm just a sucker for punishment." The girl laughed.

"Do you have a name?"

"Yes, I do. My name is Ripley. What's your name?"

"Roseway, my name is Roseway," she said lowly.

"Roseway," Ripley laughed. "That is so corny." She laughed some more.

"Well Ripley," Roseway said, laughing back. "I bet I know why your mother named you that. You are like a ripple in a shirt that you just can't get out?"

Looking offended, Ripley became quiet. Then they both looked at each other with a snarl, then broke out in laughter. Their facial expressions softened. Ripley joked, "I do believe that you have a puddle under your butt from that ice melting." They laughed contagiously. Ripley stood up on her feet, dusted off her dirty, tattered jeans, and reached out her hand to Roseway. "Can I help you to your feet?"

With a puzzled look on her face, Roseway hesitated, but then grasped Ripley's hand and Ripley pulled her up. Ripley's hand was sticky from the garbage and the pop cans. Roseway wiped her hands on her pant legs with a disgusted expression on her face. Ripley laughed again.

"Nice to meet you, Roseway. Hey, help me gather up these cans. You can help me take them to the recycle depot."

Roseway hesitated a moment and then reached down and helped Ripley with the cans. They cashed in the cans and Ripley bought a couple cheap burgers for a buck a piece and gave one to Roseway.

Ripley muttered, "There is this old, abandoned warehouse where me and a couple of friends stay. If you like, I'll introduce you to them? Maybe they will let you stay there with us for a while. I can just imagine what will happen to you if you sleep on the street. Come with me."

Ripley took Roseway down this long alleyway. Garbage cans were stacked at the back of a fast food restaurant. The smell was that of decomposing meat and maggots. Ripley grabbed Roseway's hand and pulled her along. "Hurry, we don't want anyone to see us entering the building."

Roseway felt a nervous tension build inside her stomach. For a minute she was thinking, *I don't even know this girl. Why should I trust her?*

Then a still, small voice whispered: TRUST THAT I AM WITH YOU, ROSEWAY. BELIEVE THAT I WILL DIRECT YOU TO A SHELTER AND A REFUGE. I WILL PROTECT YOU. HAVE FAITH IN THE LORD YOUR GOD.

They entered the warehouse. Uneasiness shadowed Roseway in the darkness until her eyes began to adjust. She could feel the cool dampness seep into her bones. The cement floor and walls were dingy grey, covered in graffiti. There were sleeping bags and junk scattered about the floor. In one corner was a young man sitting among his possessions, counting his change. His guitar case was full of coins. With his calloused finger tips, he rolled the coins into newspaper. A guitar leaned against the wall beside him. Ripley introduced Roseway to Jim.

"Jim, this is Roseway. Roseway, this is Jim. She is new to town, doesn't have a place to stay. Do you mind if she crashes here for a while?"

Jim's dark brown eyes brightened, as he looked her up and down like someone buying a new painting. With his Newfoundlander accent he said, "Ello darlin, I guess you can stay 'ere a while." Jim picked up his guitar and began to play an old down east tune.

Beneath the stubble on his chin and his curly brown hair was a baby-faced boy not more than nineteen. He was not much of a talker, but he expressed himself quite well with his velvet voice as the words rolled from his tongue. His smile lit up his face as he sang. Roseway couldn't help but remark on how well he sang. She tried to look into his soul while she watched and listened to him sing.

Ripley grabbed Roseway by the hand and pulled her toward her corner. "You can listen to him later. He is always singing. Here, you can share my corner with me. These are my things. We'll have to get you a sleeping bag. They give them out at the Salvation Army. But for tonight I'll share mine. Jenn keeps her things over in that corner."

"Who is Jenn?" Roseway asked.

"Jenn is a friend who stays with us. I'll tell you about her later. Mostly people just come and go all hours of the night and day. You'll get used to the disruptions. Anyway, whatever you do, don't let anyone see you come in or go out of this place, or they will kick us out of here."

It was nearing nightfall and almost everyone was out of the warehouse. Roseway just wanted to sleep. She was so exhausted from the long journey. Ripley went out and so did Jim. Jim played his guitar on the street corner and collected money. Roseway didn't know where Ripley went at night. Roseway lay on the sleeping bag and listened to the sounds of the traffic and street noise. She still missed Icon, and as she lay there, she still felt so alone. Her head was spinning with thoughts—of home, Joseph, Icon and BJ. She tried to remember her momma's face. She wondered what Billy and Susie would look like now. The pleasant thought of her family helped her drift off into sleep.

It was early in the morning, still dark except for the opening door letting in the streetlight. In came Jenn with a man, and they went to her corner. Roseway's ears perked as she listened to them. She lifted her head up over her sleeping bag. Her face flushed with disbelief as she watched the two of them. They seemed to be too preoccupied to even notice Roseway lying there. They were making a lot of noise with one another. Then Roseway pulled the sleeping bag up over her head, wondering what on earth she had gotten herself into.

Not a long time after, Jim came in. He stood for a moment looking at Roseway. Roseway felt him looking at her and pretended to be asleep. Jim scratched his head and went to his makeshift bed. A half hour later, Ripley came into the warehouse, tripping over Roseway. Ripley said a few slurring words and giggled as she slid herself into the sleeping bag alongside Roseway.

"Are you drunk, Ripley?" Roseway smelled the alcohol from Ripley's breath.

"Go back to sleep, Rose."

Roseway rolled over to face the opposite direction to try to go back to sleep. Ripley cuddled her body up against Roseway and plunked her arm over top of her. Roseway's eyes opened as she lay still, enjoying the human touch. She hadn't felt a human loving touch or a hug since Joseph. A sense of being comforted and loved washed over her to feel that physical closeness again.

"Goodnight, Ripley."

Ripley replied with a snore as she drifted off into never-never land.

Morning came quickly. Roseway quietly slipped out of the sleeping bag. When she did, Ripley grabbed her by the arm. "Where are you going?"

"I'm just going out to look around. I can't sleep."

Ripley mumbled more words and then rolled over and went back to sleep. Roseway walked the main street. Everything seemed so big to her. The buildings and the cement sidewalks seemed naked and treeless. It made her think of a big cement cemetery. People dressed in fine clothing, walking hurriedly, talking on cell phones. They all seemed like robots on a mission. No one smiled or took much notice of each other. Maybe they were too busy to smile, in a hurry to get to that next appointment. Perhaps they were caught up in their little world called self.

A rugged old man lay passed out on the sidewalk as the hot morning sun began to heat him like a fried egg. People walked over him like he was a crack in the cement. Roseway couldn't help but stare at the man, wondering if he was even alive. She bent down and shook the man's shoulder. "Hey Mister, are you all right?"

The man spoke deliriously as he grabbed her by the arm. Startled, Roseway pulled her arm out of his grip, then the man fell back to sleep.

Hunger made Roseway's stomach ache as she continued to walk. With her head down, she saw a couple of pennies lying in the gutter and picked them up. She didn't want to ask anyone for money. She was timidly estranged. There was a little market with some tables filled with fruits and vegetables. Her mouth watered looking at the fruit. She reached down and picked a shiny apple. Her teeth bit into the apple and the juice dripped down her chin. She licked her chin with her tongue and went to take another bite.

Suddenly a strong hand squeezed hard on her arm and pulled her back to the store. "What do you think you are doing, young lady? Give me that apple you stole from my table. Don't you know you have to pay for this food? I could call the police on you and have you thrown in jail."

Bewildered, Roseway didn't quite understand what she did that was so wrong. Her natural response as she shook nervously was a quick one. "I'm sorry sir. I was just really hungry."

"Why don't you get a job? Don't steal." He snapped. His words were harsh and his tone cut deep, reminding her of BJ. Cowering, Roseway put her hands over her head expecting a blow for what she did wrong. The man was dismayed by Roseway's cowering posture and her tear-filled eyes. He looked at her a little taken back. In a quieter tone of voice, he said, "Now, now girl, I'm not going to hurt you. I tell you what. You can work for me packing some groceries. I'll give you minimum wage. Would you like to earn some money?"

Roseway wiped her face and began to smile in disbelief, not fully understanding what he was offering. Somehow it sounded like the right thing to do. "Really?"

Pointing toward the table, the man said, "Okay then, you get over there and unload those boxes of vegetables onto the table, and eat this apple. You'll need some strength." He threw the apple back to her.

"Thanks, Mister. Thanks."

"The name is Mr. Duncan. Now get to work." He said with a grin.

7
SHARING

Mr. Duncan let Roseway off work around four o'clock, sending her off with a bag of fruit and vegetables. She went into the warehouse, where Ripley, Jim and Jenn were gathered.

"Where the heck have you been all day?" They asked simultaneously.

"I got a job at the grocery market on 5th Avenue."

"What is in the bag?" Jim asked as he grabbed the bag out of Roseway's arms.

"Hey, what is the big idea?" Roseway asked.

Jenn spoke up. "If you stay here, you have to share whatever you get. What money you earn goes into the pot. We all put in what we receive. That is the way it is, if you don't like it, leave."

Roseway scrunched up her face trying to process this arrangement. Seeing she had no other place to stay, she said, "Okay, but let me ask you just what each of you contribute, and who decides what to do with the money?"

Jenn replied, "That is none of your business. All that matters is that we contribute." Looking at Jim and then Ripley, Jenn spoke decisively. "I don't think she should stay here. Her minimum wage is peanuts. Besides, I don't want another person staying here. I need privacy."

"Just a minute," Ripley said. "I don't see why Rose can't stay. She is going to contribute and I want her to stay. What do you think, Jim?"

"Yeah, let her stay for a bit and let's see how things work out."

Happily, Ripley said, "It is two against one. She stays."

"Oh whatever, I have to go find some work," Jenn said, storming out.

Roseway was sensitive to barbs she felt from Jenn. "Ripley, I don't think Jenn likes me all that much. I didn't exactly get off to a good start with her. Is she always so grumpy?"

"Ah Rose, don't worry about her. She has little hissy fits once in a while. Her hair is too tightly spun, that's all. She had some hard times growing up."

Ripley quickly told Jenn's story. "Jenn is twenty years old. She left the Indian reservation when she was sixteen. Her father is an alcoholic who abused her and her sisters. She couldn't stand the weekend drinking binges. One night when Jenn turned down his advances, he kicked her out on the street. She worked her way from Vancouver to Prince George. When she was in Vancouver, she almost overdosed on ecstasy. That was when she was admitted into a drug-free program. For a while she cleaned up and it seemed she had kicked her drug addiction.

"A year later she was back out on the street and back on drugs. The drugs always seem to find her. Her drug habits lead her into prostitution. It is a quick way for her to make money to pay for her habit. Believe me; it has had an effect on her physical and emotional being. She became a tough shell of who she used to be. Like the saying goes, 'be tough, or get beat down.' So, she got tough. Jenn is a little messed up. When you get to know her, she is not that bad. The hard part is getting to know her. Stay out of her way and you'll have no trouble. I'll watch out for you, Roseway. You are my new little buddy."

Ripley put her hand on Roseway's shoulder. She smiled warmly and looked in her eyes. Roseway didn't quite know how to handle Ripley's displays of affection. At the same time, it felt good. She felt herself being swept into a friendship—a friendship like she had never experienced with anyone else.

"I think I have myself a new friend," Ripley said as she gave Roseway a gentle hug. Ripley's hug was so gentle and nurturing. Roseway remembered a familiar feeling from years ago when her mother had hugged her.

"Hey Rose, do you want to come to the public recreation center with me? I always sneak in there to shower and swim. My friend Nick always lets me in."

"That would be a great idea. After all Ripley, you sure stink like a garbage dumpster."

"I do?" Ripley's nose crinkled after smelling her shirt. "Wow. I do stink. You don't exactly smell like a flower yourself. Well then, let's get out of here."

"I don't have a swimsuit."

"We will just go to the lost and found and find you one. Let's go."

Arm in arm, they walked a couple of blocks to get to the recreation complex. They laughed and giggled as Ripley shared one funny story after another. When they arrived, Nick allowed them both to go into the change rooms. They proceeded to try on bathing suits from the lost and found. Ripley laughed hysterically when Roseway put on this one bathing suit. "You look like Ma Kettle in that thing."

"Ma who?" Roseway asked.

"That is something my Grandma might have worn a hundred years ago."

Roseway looked back with a blank look on her face. "I'd rather swim naked."

Ripley pulled a two-piece bathing suit out of the box. "You have to wear something. Here, this is more like it."

Roseway took the skimpy-looking suit and smiled. "I'll put this on."

Wrapped in a towel, she sheepishly followed Ripley to the pool. They splashed around in the water until a handsome lifeguard warned them, no splashing. For hours they swam and talked. Roseway's sentimental emotions began to flow. Choking them down, she felt a tear hug the corner of her eye as she looked at Ripley. "This is the most fun I've ever had, Ripley."

With an empathetic gaze, they just looked at each other in thoughtful retrospect.

Ripley urged, "Come on. Let's get showered and go."

They went into the change room and saw some nice clean clothes hanging in some of the unlocked lockers.

"Here Rose, put these on, they look like they are about your size. I'll wear these."

"We can't take these clothes. They belong to someone else," Roseway said with righteous conviction.

"Why do you care? Do you want to put those dirty clothes back on?"

"No, but I don't want to steal. Why don't we wash them in the Laundromat?"

"I don't have that much money today. You suit yourself. I'm taking these nice pants. Don't be such a drag, Rose."

"I'd rather be a drag than a thief, Rip. I'm going to wear my own clothes. When I get paid from Mr. Duncan, then I'll get some new clothes and wash these old ones."

Covering over her guilty conscience, Ripley said, "Oh, whatever."

The two girls headed back to the warehouse. On the way, Ripley went into a coffee shop to see a friend. She came out with a coffee. "See that guy waving? That is Danny." She pointed to the coffee shop window. Roseway could see him wave at them. He reminded her of Joseph. For a moment she thought how nice it would be to see him wave from the coffee shop window.

"Danny gives me a free coffee once in a while. Here, we'll share." Popping the lid off the coffee, she gave it a stir, took a sip and then passed the cup over to Roseway. "So Rose, what brought you here to Prince George? Where did you live before you came here?"

The coffee also reminded Roseway of Joseph. They sat on a little wooden bench at a nearby park and began to tell each other their stories. Ripley swallowed the dry lump in her throat hearing Roseway tell her story. She felt an empathetic churning within herself as her eyes stung, holding back her tears. In some ways she could relate so much to Roseway.

Ripley began to tell Roseway that she had always lived in the city. "It's all I've ever known, Rose. I come from a very rich family. I know you wouldn't think that by looking at me. My mother has all her high society friends, and she has parties all the time. My parents divorced when I was fifteen. My dad owns some conglomerate in Utah. I guess Mother fared well in the settlement. Dad took off to the States and I never saw him again. My mother would have boyfriends over all the time. Sometimes she would go away for a week and just leave my sister and me to fend for ourselves. My mother never cared for us, it seemed. She wouldn't let me have any friends over.

"Some guy raped me when I was fifteen. I got pregnant and my mother made sure I had an abortion. Heaven forbid anyone knew of our shame. Tell you the truth, I've always resented my mother so much. I hated being home, so I went out with my friends all the time. We would get high on drugs. It helped numb the reality and fill the emptiness that I felt most of the time. I guess Mother couldn't handle me, so she kicked me out of the house when I was seventeen. I had just finished high school. I've been living on the street since. Mother and I could never see eye to eye, if you know what I mean?"

"No, I guess I don't, really. Cause I never had my mother around all these years. I missed her so much that it has been all I could think of and dream about, that someday I would find my way back home to Mom and my family. Sometimes we don't know what we have until it is taken away from us. I'm not saying that you should forget your anger and hurt, or whatever it is that you feel toward your mother. Maybe try and see things from your mother's perspective. My mom always said you never know why people do the things they do, or say the things they say until you have walked a mile or two in their shoes. I'm not making excuses for your mother or the choices she made or how she treated you. Sometimes people screw up. All I'm trying to say is that maybe trying to look at life from a different perspective might help you see your mother in a different light. You have a lot to forgive. There is always hope that you could reconcile all your differences. I am sorry that you had to go through that, Ripley. I can't imagine how you must feel."

"You know what? I really like you, Rose. I like the way you say things so straight out, even if I don't agree."

They hugged each other for a moment, not saying a word. No words could express more the care and sympathy they both felt toward each other.

"Look at you, Rose. You are such a mess. Your face is all blotchy now from crying. Rose, you are such a mush ball."

"I can't help crying. I'm so emotional these days. When I was around BJ, I wasn't allowed to cry. I held in my emotions all the time, unless I went to the meadow to pray. Your story really moved me. I can't help but think how terrible it must have been for you."

"Yes, it was terrible. Anyway, I don't usually dwell on my past. Enjoy today and let tomorrow take care of itself. Besides, what good does it do me or anyone to get sad about things I had no control over? Things could always be worse. Why, I could get all mushy and cry and look like you." She laughed at her own joke, then wiped away her friend's tears.

"You're the best, Ripley."

"I know!" She said with a grin. They both laughed together.

Back to the warehouse they walked. At the warehouse they combed each other's hair and put on make-up. Ripley put make-up on herself and then on Rose.

"Ripley, I've never worn make-up before."

"No kidding, will you sit still? You keep squirming."

"Sorry! Ya know what Rip? As soon as I get some money, I'm gonna find my way home. Maybe take a bus."

"That is crazy, Rose. You don't even know where your home is."

"Well, I know it is on King Street."

"Rose you are such twit. Don't you know that every town has a King Street? By the way, what is your full name?"

"My name is Roseway."

"No duh, your last name?"

"I don't really remember my last name. I think it started with a Sha...Oh, I don't know. Maybe you could go with me, Ripley? You and me, we could ride the bus together."

"Well, Rose, that is the smartest thing you said yet. It might be kind of interesting to get out of this dump, travel, maybe make it to the coast, walk in the ocean waves and let sand flow between my toes. Ah Yeah. There is a big world out there, just waiting for Ripley Wilks and Roseway Sha...You keep that thinking cap on, Rose; maybe you'll remember your last name. That would help us find your way home."

"Ripley, are you ever going to tell me your real name?"

"Sure. It's Ripley, believe it or not." She joked again. A look of confusion came over Roseway's face not understanding Ripley's humour. She picked up a rolled pair of dirty socks and playfully threw them at Ripley. Ripley wrestled Roseway down and tickled her. They both laughed hysterically.

Jenn came in the door. "Well if it isn't twiddle-dee and twiddle-dumb. Why don't you both take a hike for a while? I've got a friend coming over in half an hour. I need about two hours."

Ripley nudged Roseway. "Come on, let's get out of here."

It was about nine o'clock in the evening. The city air was thick and warm. The night had an air of mischief hanging over the city. The city lights gave a fluorescent glow to the darkness.

8
THE UPPER ROOM

The streetlights looked like stars as they shined off the calm, glasslike water. The Fraser River floated through the city. The cooling of the late summer's night left sporadic wispy pockets of mist along the shore's edge. Roseway and Ripley walked the sidewalk along the river, and then walked back into the downtown area. As they walked the main street, they stopped in front of an old eighteenth century church. It was just a small stucco building almost lost amongst the construction of the newer buildings and big glass boutiques. A fluorescent cross on top of the church roof was a landmark glowing with light. It was set apart. The wooden doors to the church were open and Roseway was drawn to the heavenly music coming from inside. Roseway begged, "Oh, that music sounds so beautiful. Let's go inside, Ripley."

"No! I don't want to go in there. If I go into that church, it will probably fall down on me. I'm not a church girl."

"Oh, come on! Please. You believe in God, don't you?"

"Honestly Rose, I don't really think I do. If there was a God in this world, why would so many horrible things happen?"

"It is not God's fault that we humans mess it up. Oh come on, please go inside with me?"

Roseway yanked Ripley by the arm, and inside they ventured.

Up at the front of the church was a big banner which read, "Welcome to the Upper Room." Inside was a group of people clapping their hands, dancing and singing with all their hearts. The smiles on their faces were enchantingly joyful. When the song ended they all praised Jesus with Hallelujahs and an Amen. "Praise Jesus, Hallelujah!"

Roseway felt such a presence of Holiness. Ripley thought it was all very strange. After the singing, a white-haired man stood up at the front of the church and introduced himself as Pastor Ken. He spoke reverently about the presence of God. Roseway clung to every word he spoke.

Ripley tugged at Roseway. "Come on, let's go." But Roseway wanted to stay. "Rose, I'm leaving. I can't stand this stuff. I'll see you at the warehouse later."

"Please don't go. Stay just a little longer."

The conviction Ripley was feeling was something she did not want to handle. "No, I have had enough. I'm going over to the Cancun. I'll see you later." Ripley snuck out of the doors at the back of the church. Roseway stayed and listened attentively as the Pastor spoke a sermon about the Father's love.

Pastor Ken continued, "God is your Father, your Abba Daddy. He loves you so much. He cares for you and loves you more than your earthly dad ever could. God's love is eternal, forgiving and full of grace and mercy. An example of a father's love is found in the story of the prodigal son. This son was from a wealthy family. He asked his father for his inheritance. The son took all the money and belongings his father gave to him and he went away.

"When he was away, the son spent all his money on things he wanted and had a really good time. Then his money was all gone, his friends deserted him and he became homeless and had to scrounge for food. He finally found work cleaning out pigpens. His life of wealth and comfort had changed. He went from having everything a person could want or need to someone who had nothing.

"One day, when he found himself eating table scraps with the pigs, he realized what he had lost, and then he ventured home. This son had been so humbled. When he arrived home, he fell before his father's feet. He said to his father, 'I am not worthy to be your son, for I have sinned and I am not worthy to wear your name. Let me work as your servant.'

"The father cried and was overjoyed to see his son return home. He hugged his son and welcomed him home. He said to his son, 'My son, my son, you were lost and now you are found. You were dead, but now you are alive.' The father forgave his son and took him back home. God's love toward us is similar to the love this father demonstrated toward his son—a son who had broken all the rules and went against the protocol of their family's biblical standards."

Roseway couldn't believe the sermon. The prodigal son sounded so much like her new friend Ripley. Oh how she wished Ripley had stayed and listened to the story. Maybe she would go home to her mother. The parallel was so similar. At the same time, the sermon also made Roseway think of her home again. It made her wonder who her father was. She wanted so much to find her home. It almost felt like an impossible hope. It made her feel so frustrated and tired from trying, thinking and hoping about it so much. Her heart even felt weak from the journey. As her thoughts drifted in and out, she continued to listen to this wise man at the front of the church.

"There is someone here tonight who has felt they have never had a father. You have been abused and feel so hurt inside. There is someone here who feels like they have done such horrible things, they cannot be forgiven. You are caught in the prison of self. If that person is you, then come up to the front and allow God the Father to touch you and heal your pain. He can set you free from the fowler's snare."

Roseway's throat tightened. Her heart was pounding through her chest. She could feel the sweat roll from her armpits. Like a jack rabbit she suddenly jumped up from her seat. The calling to go forward was so strong. With burning eyes, she walked to the front of the church and fell on her knees, collapsing like a rag doll. She sobbed and sobbed as a river of uncontrollable tears soaked into the church floor. Pastor Ken reached down and put his arm around her. Roseway allowed her head to fall into his shoulder as she continued to weep.

The Pastor said to Roseway, "Young lady, God loves you so much. He is going to do something in your life—something so amazing you won't believe it, even if you were to see it."

Roseway's eyes opened with a questioning look. Pastor Ken helped her up off the floor as her tears subsided. She went back to her seat on the wooden pew. Shortly after that the service ended.

People introduced themselves to Roseway and made her feel welcome to return any time. Roseway left feeling like the weight of the world had been lifted from her shoulders. She felt like she could almost walk on water. Her faith had been ignited like never before. The permanent smile on her face lit up her eyes. As she walked back to the warehouse, she daydreamed and wondered what Pastor Ken meant by what he'd said. What was the awesome thing God was going to do? She felt like bursting out in song with her own hallelujahs.

She slipped quietly into the warehouse. No one was there to tell about her exciting experience. Into her sleeping bag she snuggled, listening to the night noises outside. She looked up and smiled and prayed to God, Thank you, Father, for loving me. Thank you for tonight. I love you, Lord. She drifted into a deep sleep and began to dream.

9
The Cabin Fire

Roseway found herself back in time, in the haunting memories of the cabin and the last day she saw Big Joe. The potbelly stove was red with heat. Sometimes the nights cooled, bringing an early frost. By the month of August, the mountain temperatures fluctuated from warm or hot days to very cold nights. She remembered that last day at the cabin. The previous night was cold outside. Big Joe lit the fire. The chimney pipe glowed in the darkness like red-hot coal. It brought warmth to the cabin.

When the sun began to rise, BJ went over to Roseway's cot and pulled the pillow out from under her head. "Wake up, lazy!" He rasped at her. "We need some water for breakfast. Go down to da stream and bring up a bucket of water." Roseway pulled the blanket up over her head. Big Joe yanked the blanket off of her, grabbed her by the hair and pulled her to her feet. "Get going."

Roseway stared back at him like darts were shooting from her eyes. She had such hatred inside her toward him. Her thoughts were murderous. I wish he were dead.

"Did you say something?" he asked.

"No!" She replied with her head down, looking to the floor.

"Then get dat water. Hurry up."

Roseway wiped the sleep from her eyes and grabbed the tin bucket and made her way down to the stream. The thoughts in her head were turning like a potter's wheel. I've got to get out of this place. It is madness. He is madness. The fear he breathes into me is like a fire of locusts eating away at my flesh. I've got to do something. I can't take it anymore. She took the water back to the cabin. Big Joe made breakfast—some cornmeal porridge and scones.

They had a few wild turkeys they kept in a small pen and a cow they used for milking. Joe was a very resourceful man who didn't waste anything. One thing he did right was teaching Roseway survival skills. Now Roseway felt she was ready to use them. After breakfast, BJ told Roseway to clean up the dishes, and then he had some weeding for her to do in the garden. Roseway was always afraid to talk back, but this day her mouth spewed before she could bite her tongue.

"No, I'll not be your slave any longer." Then she bit her lip so as not to say more. Big Joe was standing by the wood stove with the door open. He was throwing wood into the stove one piece after the other. He was flabbergasted at Roseway's disobedience. He just kept throwing in wood while his blood began to boil along with the pot of water on the stove. The veins on his neck pulsed and his face reddened as he stood and walked toward Roseway. She stood fear-struck with anticipation.

"What did you just say to me?" Big Joe said, waiting for a recantation.

Roseway spoke quietly. "I said, I am not your slave."

She could see his blood pressure rise as his eyes widened like saucers. That dreaded hand struck like a deadly snakebite across the side of her head. The force knocked her off her feet and flying onto his bed. He leaped on top of her like a lion to its prey. Roseway screamed, "Please get off me. Don't hurt me!" As she screamed, his anger raged. He put his big hand over her mouth and the other around her throat. A feeling of overwhelming helplessness and panic flowed through Roseway as she tried to gasp for breath. Darkness closed in on her like evil waves. Numbness tingled through her body as she began fading out. All she could do was think to herself, Jesus, Jesus, help me, Jesus.

Big Joe released his grip when he realized what he was doing. His raspy voice yelled, "Roseway, wake up!" He shook her limp body, afraid of what he had done. The colour started to flush into her face as she gasped for breath. Tears rolled from her bloodshot eyes and he raised her up to her feet. "Drink dis water." He gestured as he poured some water into a glass. She sipped gently as her throat burned with pain. Big Joe seemed attentive to help her, realizing his lack of control moments earlier.

Going through Roseway's mind was the word escape. Her breath had returned and the strength re-entered her body. The hatred she felt within herself rose up like a combustible engine ready to blow. Looking at him, everything seemed magnified and moving in slow motion. The little cabin seemed to be in a haze as heat from the stove floated like waves. She just wanted to run away—as far away from him and the cabin as she could go. However, the thought made her entire body tremble. The last time she tried to run away, he had beat her black and blue.

Big Joe lit a cigarette and blew a puff of smoke, then bent down to stoke the fire in the stove using an iron poker. "Dis stove is getting way too hot," Big Joe muttered.

Roseway's hand shook nervously as she picked up a cast iron pan, lifted it above her head, and with all her strength hit Big Joe over the head. She heard the crack of his skull and watched his big body fall in slow motion onto the floor in front of the stove. He lay deathly still. Wide-eyed, she looked at him in a hypnotic daze, thinking that she had just killed him. She pushed him with her foot, but he did not move. Roseway ran out of the cabin as fast as she could.

Then her dream flashed back to the meadow of tranquility and the buttercup she had destroyed. Much like a replayed video, Roseway could clearly see the buttercup fall to the ground.

The dream flashed to another familiar place—she was back at the stream where the little silver fish was flip-flopping around. She remembered not helping the fish. Still caught in this dream, she remembered a voice within, telling her that Big Joe is like that fish and you should go back to the cabin and see if Big Joe is all right. Next, she was walking the path back toward the cabin. Flames lit the night path. The cabin fell to the ground. Again, the dark shadow running from the cabin made her toss in her sleep. Then she heard the whisper of Big Joe's voice: "I'm back." Roseway felt a hand on her arm as she awoke screaming, cold sweat beading her forehead and her heart pounding. In a moment of confusion she flailed at Jim as she awoke from her dream.

"Calm down, Rose. It's me, Jim. Are you all right?"

He grabbed her arms and held them tight until she realized that she was having a bad dream. Jim gasped at Roseway. "Wow, that was some trip, some nightmare you were having."

Her body felt limp, heart pounding and her shirt soaked; she leaned on Jim for a minute. Jim hugged her back. When Roseway finally regained her composure, she began to calm down.

"Thanks Jim, I'm okay now. I just had a terrible dream. That is all."

She faked a smile. Deep down, Roseway couldn't shake the reality of truth in that dream. Her thoughts invaded her mind. I killed Big Joe. I'm a murderer. If anyone knew, I would go to prison for a long time. I wish I could tell someone the truth of what I've done. How can I do that? Going to the police is out of the question.

Her dream almost overshadowed the message she had heard the night before at the Upper Room. She whispered under her breath, "No, No, I have to go to the police and tell them what happened. That is the only way I will really be free. Pay the consequences for my sin. Maybe Ripley will go with me."

"Did you say something?" Jim asked.

Flustering, Roseway responded, "Jim, where is Ripley? She is not back yet?"

"What are you, her mother now?"

"No, just wondering. Where does she go until this early in the morning?"

"Well, she usually goes to the Cancun nightclub over on Queen Street. It is a lively, high-kicking dance spot. She dances for tips, or should I say for kicks." Jim laughed.

Roseway was thinking out loud. "I'm going to take a walk. I can't sleep now. I need to clear my head."

"Would you like some company?" Jim asked with a raised eyebrow.

"No, that is okay. Thanks, though."

Roseway walked the cool streets down toward the Cancun, hoping she'd meet up with Ripley along the way. She desperately wanted to talk to her. She felt a sense of urgency within. There was an eerie air about the night, and she had a creepy sense she was being followed. Maybe I should have let Jim come along, she thought. The streets were very quiet this early in the morning. Not much action in the Cancun. Roseway knocked on the front door. She could see someone sweeping up the joint. She pounded on the door until the sweeper came and unlocked it.

"The place is closed, can't you read the sign? What do you want?"

"I'm looking for a blonde girl, pretty with blue eyes; she works as a dancer here. Have ya seen her?"

"There are a lot of blondes around here."

"Her name is Ripley."

"Oh, Ripley, well, she left about an hour ago. She was with this rugged-looking man, had a scar on his weatherworn face. Never seen him before, he was a mean looking dude. I thought maybe it was her dad. Anyway, she left and he seemed to follow her out the door."

Roseway's heart sank into her stomach. It couldn't be. Oh my God. No! Roseway ran out of the Cancun, yelling Ripley's name as she scurried down the street back toward the warehouse. She felt panic within her chest as she ran as fast as she could. At each side street alley, she slowed her pace to take a look to see if Ripley was there. Roseway had a sixth sense that she would find Ripley, and that the outcome would not be pleasant. She feared for Ripley's life. At the corner of Queen and Duke Street, she heard a noise from the alleyway. Cautiously, Roseway walked toward the darkness.

"Ripley, is that you?" She edged her way down the alley. Some garbage cans fell over, startling her, making her scream. In the dark, car headlights illuminated the eyes of a couple of raccoons.

Roseway ran out of the alleyway. Piercing the darkness with each stride, she breathed intensely as she neared the back alley that lead to the warehouse. She tripped over a box of garbage just outside the door. Then she heard moans coming from the darkness. Roseway was afraid to look, fearing it was Ripley. But she crawled toward the sounds, eyes wide and nervous. Her mouth opened, awestruck by the sight.

It was Ripley, lying in amongst the garbage, beaten and bruised. She was bleeding from her mouth and her eyes were swollen shut.

"Ripley, it's me, Rose."

Half-conscious, Ripley struggled to speak. "I'm here." Roseway touch her hand, tears rolling down her cheeks. "Who did this to you? Who would do such a thing?" She asked, afraid of the answer.

Ripley coughed as the blood trickled down the back of her throat. Roseway petted Ripley's bloody hair. Ripley squeezed Roseway's hand, acknowledging her presence. She tried to lift her head but winced at the pain. Roseway drew her head close to Ripley, praying, "Oh God, please don't take her away, too. Please help her, Lord. Hang in there, Ripley. You are going to be fine. Don't you leave me! You are the only real friend I've ever had."

Ripley whispered, "Run Rose, Big Joe...here. He . . ." Ripley lost consciousness.

Roseway yelled at the top of her lungs. "Help!"

Jim and Jenn came running out of the warehouse. Jim took one look and ran for help. Within minutes, an ambulance came to the scene and then a police car. Roseway didn't want to leave Ripley's side. She wouldn't let go of Ripley's hand. The paramedic grabbed her hand and gently released her grip. Roseway was sobbing uncontrollably as they lifted Ripley on a stretcher and put her in the ambulance. Roseway screamed and wanted to go with her. A police officer held her back, wrapping his arms around her while she kicked and screamed.

Jim and Jenn stared, dumbfounded. The police asked Jim and Jenn questions. They knew nothing about what had happened. The police took their names and let them go. Roseway was hysterical and not making much sense as she blurted out so much information. Her thoughts were scattered by her emotional break-down. No, BJ died in the fire. Ripley is going to die. It's my fault. Where is Momma? What do I do? BJ is alive. He will find Momma, Billy and Suzie and hurt them, too. He said he would do that if I ran away. He knows where they live. I have to warn them, but I don't know where they are. Listen to me. I don't feel so good. Roseway collapsed in shock. Police quickly sent for another ambulance to transport Roseway to the ER for a psychiatric evaluation.

10
THE GLASS BUBBLE

The air brakes on the tractor-trailer of Joseph's truck swished as he came to a stop in front of the police station. Joseph had dropped off his load of cargo and headed into Prince George to follow his dream. He went into the RCMP detachment to find out if they had made any progress in finding Rose Shaffer.

Police told Joseph that they had spoken with her family. They had a picture of her which was taken when she was six years old. With that picture, they made a computerized simulation of what she would look like today. When Joseph looked at the picture, he identified her as being the same Roseway he had picked up on the roadside. The police said they had not made any progress in finding her. Joseph asked if he could have a copy of the picture to place on the back of his truck, in hope that other truckers would also place her picture as a child-find photo on the back of their trucks.

Joseph left the detachment and drove around the streets of Prince George. He noticed the same little church with the steeple on top, which had been in his dream. He went in and talked to the pastor at the church. He asked him if he had seen this young girl. He showed him the picture. The pastor affirmed that yes, only a few days ago she had come in off the street and sat in on his service.

He told Joseph how upset this young girl was; that when she left she seemed to be in a high spirit. He had not seen her since.

Joseph felt excited that he was so close. He walked the street showing the picture. Some had recognized her but didn't know where she stayed. When he entered the little grocery market store, he talked to one of the grocery baggers. "Yes, I know her. That is Roseway. She works here."

Joseph smiled from ear to ear. "Where is she?" He asked with excitement.

"Don't know? Maybe Mr. Duncan knows. Ask him, he is standing over there."

Joseph approached the kind-looking man. "Hello, Mr. Duncan, I'm a friend of Roseway's, the girl in this picture."

"Is that right? Where is she? She was supposed to be working yesterday and today and I haven't seen hide or hair of her."

"Oh," Joseph grunted. "Do you know where she is staying?"

"Some old warehouse a couple blocks down. Go toward the alley at Queen and Duke Street. It's that dingy warehouse at the end of the alley. It is scheduled for demolition soon."

"Thanks, Mr. Duncan, thank you."

Joseph ran down the street kicking his heels, happy as a songbird. When he got down to Duke Street, he walked down the alley and recognized the warehouse as Mr. Duncan had described it. He knocked on the outside door, but no one answered. He opened the door and slowly walked inside. When he closed the door behind him, he was grabbed from behind. A strong arm wrapped around his chest and a knife blade rested on Joseph's throat.

"What are you doing in here? Who are you?" Jim asked in a defensive voice.

"Wow, take it easy. I'm just looking for a friend, Roseway."

The knife tightened on his neck. "What do you want with her?"

"I just want to help her get home."

"How do you know Roseway?"

"My name is Joseph. I picked her up on the roadside over a year ago. We drove a long way together and she told me her story. I wanted to make sure she would get home safe."

Jim loosened the grip on Joseph. "Roseway mentioned you. They took Roseway away two nights ago. Some guy beat our friend Ripley up so bad that she is in the hospital in a coma. Roseway found her in the alley. When they took Ripley away, Roseway went crazy, lost it. Police had an ambulance come and take her to the hospital, too. I think she is on the nut ward."

Joseph raced out of the warehouse and made his way to the hospital, breaking speed limits along the way. He went in and asked the nurse at the admitting desk if there was a girl named Roseway admitted two nights ago. She told him that there was a confidentiality law and she could not give any information without family identification.

Joseph called the police and told them Roseway was at the hospital and asked them to send someone over to investigate. Police identified and confirmed that Rose Shaffer was the girl admitted to the hospital. They contacted the family and they said they would drive from their home in Kelowna. It was at least a ten-hour drive.

Meanwhile, police told Joseph that Roseway had had a severe mental breakdown, and that she had been heavily sedated. Joseph persuaded the officer to allow him to see her. They did so with a police escort at the door.

Joseph walked down the hall. It seemed like a glass bubble with reinforced glass doors and windows. The lump in his throat tightened with each step toward her room. Roseway lay sleeping. A tear rested in the corner of his eye as he looked at her lying there with her arms fastened to the bed. He pulled a chair up beside her bed, touched her hand softly, leaned over and kissed her cheek. Then he sat in his chair and began to pray.

"Lord Jesus, thank you for helping me to find her. Please Lord, bring healing to her mind and set her free from the bondage of her past. Help her to take every thought and fear captive to the power of Christ. Please show me how I can help her through this process. Amen!"

MY SON JOSEPH, CONTINUE TO BE HER FRIEND. LET HER KNOW YOU CARE ABOUT HOW SHE FEELS. CONTINUE TO SHOW YOUR LOVE TOWARD HER. ROSE WILL FIND THE WAY TO FREEDOM.

Roseway awoke pulling at her arms, trying to break free from the straps. She screamed, "Let me out of here!"

Joseph stepped back and a nurse came in with a syringe to tranquillize her.

Joseph interrupted. "Wait! Please don't give that to her." He stood up beside Roseway and looked at her panic-stricken face and fear-filled eyes.

He spoke softly to her. "Roseway, calm down, it is me, Joseph. Shh, you are safe. I'm with you. I'm not going to leave you. It's okay. Your family is coming to see you, Rose."

Roseway felt an anxious flow run through her body. Joseph asked the nurses to take off the restraints. He whispered to Roseway, "Keep calm, Roseway, and we will get these things off of you. Shh, everything will be okay." Roseway quieted and became peaceful. The nurse allowed Joseph to gently untie the restraints.

"Joseph, I can't believe you are here. Please tell me I'm not dreaming."

"You are not dreaming, Rose. I'm really here. Everything will be alright."

Still a little groggy from being medicated, Roseway asked, "How is Ripley?"

"They are taking good care of her. She is upstairs. Let's concentrate on getting you better." Joseph didn't want to upset her by telling her how critical Ripley's condition was at this time.

Roseway's thoughts began to clear. She felt an urgency to explain what happened, knowing that there was still a threat over her family's lives. She began to blurt out her thoughts to Joseph. "There is nothing wrong with me. We have got to get out of here, though. Big Joe is coming back. He hurt Ripley because of me. He will hurt my family, you or anyone I care about."

"Big Joe is dead. He died in the cabin fire. Do you remember?"

With a tense tone of agitation, Roseway said, "No no no, you don't understand. He is alive. He beat up Ripley!"

Worried at the momentum of Roseway's hysterics, the nurse injected the tranquillizer into Roseway's arm.

"Ouch, don't do that . . ." Roseway snapped as she fought to stay awake. "Please no, you don't understand. . ."

Joseph rebuked the nurse. "Why did you do that? She was trying to tell me something."

The nurse responded, "She was getting too hysterical again. That is not good for her when she is recovering from such an emotional trauma. Let her get some rest. You can talk to her later. Go on now. You shouldn't even be in here. We will watch her."

11
MEMORIES

Joseph paced back and forth in the waiting room all day until Roseway's family arrived at the hospital. Corporal Higgins accompanied the family as they walked down the long hallway to where Joseph was standing. Corporal Higgins introduced them to each other. "Joseph, this is Roseway's mother, Noreen Shaffer, sister Sue and her brother Bill. Everyone, this is Joseph. Joseph is the one who helped us find your daughter."

Joseph smiled. "Nice to meet all of you. Roseway has told me much about you. She will be so happy to see you again."

Rose's mother Noreen was a soft-featured woman dressed in a light sport jacket and a long blue-jean skirt that draped over her shoes. She rubbed her sweaty palms on her dress, occasionally running her fingers through her short brown hair as they talked. Instinctively she surged forward and hugged Joseph tightly, thanking him profusely. "Thank you so much, Joseph, for what you have done. We are all so grateful. How can I ever repay you for finding my daughter?"

"I'm just glad to see that Roseway will finally be back with her family."

"Don't you mean Rose, not Roseway?"

"She now prefers to be called Roseway," Joseph replied.

Noreen lowered her brows and shook her head. "When can I see my Rose?" She asked anxiously.

"Roseway has been heavily sedated since they brought her in. Just to caution you, Roseway had some kind of emotional breakdown and she has been sedated to keep her calm. Maybe she will be awakening soon. Have a seat and I'll go see if you can see her now."

Noreen sat in a cold steel armchair, sighing with relief. Her mind drifted off, remembering back to when Roseway was a little baby. Memories of the cold delivery room invaded her thoughts, reminding her of all the mixed feelings she had felt. The pain of childbirth had not been new to her, having given birth to Susie and Billy first. As the contractions had increased to every thirty seconds, she had felt her skin stretch, the pain ever so real.

Billy and Susie's father had died in a car accident, shortly after Billy was born. Noreen had to work nights at a diner to provide for the children. Her feelings were mixed about having another child, another mouth to feed. She often wondered how she could afford another child. The biggest obstacle she had to get past was the way she had conceived Roseway.

The local diner was the hot spot for a cheap meal. All the locals went there for a bite to eat, to chat and get caught up on the local gossip— like who was Henry Shawbrook sleeping with this week? What about that Mable Spencer, she was sporting a nice black eye the other day. That old drunk of a husband always beats her when he goes home drunk, then they are out at church on Sunday telling some tale of how the dog lifted its head when she was playing with it and it smacked her right in the nose.

A transient traveler frequently visited the diner. He took a fancy to Noreen Shaffer. Why not? She was single, friendly, and a quite attractive young woman. But then again she was friendly with all the customers. This man was an odd fellow, a loner. His left eye was lighter than his right. He had black shaggy hair, tanned skin—an outdoors man. He made Ms. Shaffer a little uncomfortable as time went on. His constant visits to the diner seemed a little obsessive, as he always had to be waited on by her. She felt like she was being watched all the time.

She remembered the night clearly. It was her turn to close up the diner. Noreen went through the regular routine of scraping off the grills and mopping the floor, and then put the closed sign in the window. Everyone else had left for the evening. It was about midnight. She turned out the lights and closed the door behind her and was just about to lock the front door. Suddenly she felt a hand caress her arm and his body up against her back. His warm breath made the hairs on her neck prickle when he whispered, "Hello darlin. How bout you make me a coffee before ya close up for da night?"

It was a raspy low tone of voice. Noreen felt chills run down her spine.

"Sir, the diner closes now. I have to get home to my children. I have a babysitter waiting for me."

"Come on Noreen, won't take but a couple minutes."

He put his hand over hers as it rested on the doorknob. He twisted her hand and the door knob until it opened. He nudged her forward, back into the diner. Noreen turned around and looked at his face. The moon's ray shone through the diner window.

She gasped. "It is you. Joe is your name, right?"

"Yeah, dat's right 'oney," he said with his Newfoundlander accent, wearing a proud smile as he moved closer to her. "You are a very beautiful woman, Noreen."

Nervously, Noreen tried to appease Joe about the complement. "Well, thank you, Joe. Look, I'll make a coffee, but then I really must go home." She plugged in the kettle. "Is instant coffee okay?"

"Dat would be great. Why don't ya come and sit down wit me til da kettle boils?"

He reached over the counter and grabbed her by the arm.

"Hey! Don't do that. Get your hand off of me." She pushed his hand off of her, then rubbed her arm where he had gripped it.

"Now is dat any way ta treat your customers? I was just being friendly." Joe got up off of his stool and walked around the counter to where Noreen was standing waiting for the kettle to boil. She could feel her heart pound as her hands shook with fear.

"Customers are not allowed behind the counter. Your coffee will be ready any minute. Why don't you go sit over there and I'll bring it to you?"

He kept walking toward her. "I've ad my eye on ya for quite some time. I really like ya. How about you and I go out some time? I know you like me too. You ave been so friendly ta me. I've seen your flirtatious looks at me."

While stirring his coffee, she replied, "Joe, you are making me uncomfortable. I don't even know you. Please go sit down over there."

The colour in his face reddened. He became a little more aggressive. "Noreen, I tink I'm in love wit you," he stuttered, as he stepped closer to her.

Noreen pushed him back from her. "I don't know what to say. I don't want to hurt your feelings, but I don't love you. I don't even know you, so please back off."

Her rejection inflamed him with anger. He grabbed her and pulled her close. She struggled to pull herself away. "Let me go!"

He was strong and his hand squeezed even harder into her arm. She managed to grab the hot cup of coffee and poured it on him. He yelled at the pain and for a second loosened his grip. Noreen tried to run out from behind the counter, but he lunged at her, knocking her to the floor. She tried to scream, but he put his hand over her mouth as he sat on top of her. With one free hand she reached to his face and with her long nails scratched, ripping into his flesh. Enraged, he instinctively hit her in the face, almost knocking her unconscious. A blur of dizziness made the room spin in slow motion. "Now dat is more like it darlin. Just relax."

She felt helplessness, feeling his body on top of her. Next thing she knew she awoke and the police were talking to her. She didn't hear a word they were saying as they wheeled her to an ambulance. There was no sign of Joe anywhere.

Her memories then flashed to the birth of her little baby girl nine months later. She remembered them wrapping her newborn baby in a little pink flannelette blanket. As if it were yesterday, the image of looking at the baby for the first time erased any hesitation of not loving this little one. She looked at her and said, "You are my little Rose, such a beautiful flower in my life."

The love she instantly felt for this baby was unbreakable—a mother's bond to her child like an invisible cord. All those years, she never gave up hoping and praying that someday her little girl would be found alive. Every time the phone rang she wanted it to be Roseway or the police with good news. Each wrong phone number left a disappointment that tried to chisel her faith down to the bone. There was anger toward God that she cradled deep within. Why didn't God answer her prayers right away? Why did he allow any of this into their lives? Why would God give the gift of a child only to take her away? She didn't know the why to her questions. Most of the biblical advice that her friends tried to give her fell on deaf ears. None of their answers brought Roseway home; none of the advice changed a darn thing. It certainly didn't take away the ache she felt in her soul. Nothing filled the empty place in her heart where Roseway should be. The years apart had to be lived without

Rose. All the birthdays and events Noreen enjoyed with Susie and Billy always reminded her of what she had missed not having Rose. There were doubt storms over the years when her faith and hope seemed to diminish. Surely it was a testing of faith no one would ever want to take. The years without her flipped through her mind as she sat in that room waiting and wondering what Roseway endured during those years. Her imagination left the hairs on her arm standing straight and cold.

"Ms. Shaffer...Ms. Shaffer...You can go in and see Rose now."

Noreen snapped herself back to the present. Her heart pounded. This was the moment she had hoped and prayed to happen for such a long time. She walked anxiously down the hall toward Roseway's room. Her throat tightened from the dry lump. Noreen quickened her pace, then stopped at the door, trying to keep her eyes from watering. Thoughts invaded her mind. Will she remember me? What does she look like now? It has been such a long time.

The door squeaked as she quietly opened it. For a moment she just stood there in awe of this young woman lying in the bed. Roseway had her eyes closed and looked so peaceful with the covers pulled up over her. Noreen took baby steps toward her. Leaning over her, she whispered, "Rose, my sweet little Rose." Then she put her hand on her daughter's hand and caressed it gently. Roseway's eyes fought to open, still groggy from the medication.

"Momma," Roseway said, her eyes blurred by tears. "Oh my God, is it really you, Momma?"

She began to sob as her mother reached down and kissed her cheek, then her lips. "Yes, my baby. Your momma is here."

Roseway wrapped her arms around her so tight and just cried and cried. "I can't believe it's really you. Mom, I prayed every day that I would find my way home again. But Big Joe . . ."

"Shh, baby. You don't have to talk about Big Joe right now. Everything is going to be fine."

Noreen didn't know how she would ever tell Rose that Big Joe was actually her father. She didn't want to face the past or the memory of him. Noreen despised the man and at that moment if she could have gotten her hands on him, truly her Christian values would have gone by the wayside. She just wanted to hold her daughter and love and comfort her. "We are going to take you home with us. Billy and Sue are here, too. We just want to take you home and catch up on all these years you've been gone. We love you, Rose. We love you so much. We're so thankful we found you."

"Oh Mom, can I see Billy and Suzie? I've missed them so much."

"Yes, but the first thing I want to know is who is this young man who found you?"

"Oh, Joseph is a truck driver who picked me up off the side of the road sometime last year. It is a long story, Mom."

"I think this Joseph cares for you very much."

Roseway blushed. "Mom." A smile enveloped her flushed face. Then the door swung open and sheepishly in walked Billy and Suzie. They all hugged each other, laughing and crying at the same time.

"Where have you been all this time?"

"Did he hurt you?"

The barrage of questions fired one after the other. Ms. Shaffer blurted, "Stop, enough questions. Rose will tell us later when she is ready to talk about this. This is not the time."

Excited, Roseway said, "Suzie, or should I say Sue? Your name is not the only thing that has changed; Wow, the two of you have really changed. You've both grown up. You look so different now. It must have been Mom's home-baked beans. All that gas sprouted you right up."

"You have changed, too!" Sue replied. "You don't even look the same."

Anxious, Roseway asked, "When can I get out of this place?"

Her mother replied, "The police want to talk to you and then maybe in a week or so we will be able to take you home."

They had a long talk until visiting hours were over. They said their goodnights. Noreen, Bill and Sue left the hospital and stayed at the nearest hotel. They assured Roseway they would be back tomorrow.

12
THE REUNION

Ripley's mother, Ms. Annalisa Wilks, and Ripley's sister, Lauren, sat in the waiting room outside of the intensive care unit. Ms. Wilks had her long legs crossed, and she was dressed in a tailor-made blue wool suit, looking like she just stepped out of a fashion magazine. Her French manicured hands fidgeted with her leather handbag, and then she freshened up her lipstick. Lauren sat across the room. The tension in the room was thick like smoke. Lauren was a tall, bleached blonde with very distinctive features, high cheekbones and thick, plum-coloured lips. She was dressed in a Bloomingdale's suit. Her ocean blue eyes were fixed in a hypnotic gaze looking down at the disinfected tile floor.

The sound of the hospital door swinging open and banging against the wall interrupted the silence in the room. Looking like someone ready to go to the next emergency, a man walked with a quick pace toward them. His face was focused and stern. He was a man on a mission. A mission he had taken numerous times before.

With a self controlled tone in his voice, he introduced himself. "Hello, I'm Doctor Spandecker." With a list of medical facts pertaining to Ripley's condition, he continued. "I'm the neurologist at the hospital. I'm sorry to tell you that your daughter is in serious condition. Three days ago, Ripley was rushed into emergency after being severely beaten. She has a severe concussion, a few broken ribs causing some internal bleeding. Her nose is broken. Trauma to her face has caused bruising and swelling.

"I am mainly concerned with the swelling of her brain. X-rays showed that Ripley banged the back of her head. I believe the impact is what has caused the concussion and a severe cranial skull fracture. We can only hope that the swelling will shrink and that there is no permanent brain damage. We are treating her to try and reduce the swelling on her brain. We had to stitch the back of her head and insert a small metal plate to repair the fracture to her skull. To do this, we had to shave the hair around that area. The bad news is that she is in a coma. Hopefully she comes out of her coma sooner, rather than later. At this point we just have to wait and give her body a chance to heal."

More frustrated and worried for Ripley than she was angry at the doctor, Lauren blurted with a little sarcasm, "Well, thank you for that direct diagnosis." For years, Lauren had put up with contention within the family. As far as she was concerned, that is what brought them to that hospital room. Years of bottled up emotions were ripping at Lauren's insides like bear claws to flesh, and Dr. Spandecker seemed like the winning candidate for her to release some of that frustration.

Ms. Wilks asked, "Who did this to my daughter?"

Dr. Spandecker took a deep breath, stiffened and paused, then said, "I don't know…ah, you will have to talk to the police about that. I'll let you know as soon as her condition changes. We will monitor her condition closely and I will talk with you later today and give you an update. If you would like to go in and see Ripley, you may go in one at a time. " Spandecker exited the waiting room in the same quick manner he had entered it.

Lauren went in first, while Ms. Wilks stayed in the waiting room. For a few moments there was silence. Lauren looked at her sister and choked back any emotion. Ripley was barely recognizable with the bruising and swelling to her face. Lauren spoke softly to her, keeping a distance from the bed. Trying to break her worry and inner tension, she spoke to Ripley about memories of their past. "Hey there, little sister, you have to keep fighting, Rip. Remember, you are as stubborn as an ox. No one is more stubborn than you. Now, smarten up and come out of that coma."

The room remained silent as she paused. She wanted to see Ripley sit up in the bed right then and there. The quiet was too much. "Hey Rip, do you remember the time when you were about five and I was ten? You wanted to eat that bag of candy Uncle Bernie gave you, right before supper. Mother said no and took away the candy. You started to cry and scream, then you held your breath until you fainted. I thought Mother was going to have a conniption fit."

Lauren continued to fill the quiet by remembering good times—stories to break her sadness. "What about the time you kept asking for a glass of milk, then when Mother gave it to you, you said you didn't want it? Then when she took it away, you said you did want it. You had Mother going in circles and made her so frustrated that she poured the milk on your head. The look of shock on your face was so funny. Then you held your breath again. You got Mother back, didn't you? Probably because you knew when you did that, it made her upset.

"Girl, you are as stubborn as they get. Remember the week we stayed at the house together, by ourselves? Mother went on her little fling for a week. You took it upon yourself to make pancakes for breakfast. You put the eggs in with the flour—shells and all, and then you proceeded to cook them on high temperature. It's a miracle you didn't burn the place down. We put out the fire though, didn't we? We will put out this fire, too.

"Rip, I'm sorry I wasn't a better sister to you. We had to grow up so fast, didn't we? When you were little, I thought you were more of a pain in the butt than anything. I didn't want my bratty little sister hanging around me all the time. I think I resented having to play the mother role so much. Many times I didn't treat you very nice. I'm sorry for that, Rip. Being five years older than you was a lot of years, then. Funny, it doesn't make much difference now. Anyway kid, you just have to fight your way back to us. You have to. You've always been a fighter. Don't stop fighting now. God knows I need a little sister in my life. Don't you dare leave me here alone with Mother.

"I guess Mother will come in to see you now. You know her, always chomping at the bit." Lauren went silent and stared at Ripley. She felt like she was talking to the wall. Seeing no response from Ripley pained her heart. The frustration in her continued to build with the desperation she felt. "God! I don't know what else to say. For once, will you give us a little help here?"

Lauren sat quietly with her head bowed for a few more minutes, swallowing the lump in her throat. She hesitantly squeezed Ripley's hand, and then walked out of her room and entered the waiting area. Face to face with her mother, like the breaking of a dam, a lifetime of bottled up words and emotions flowed from her lips. Angrily she spit her words to her mother.

"Mother, this is entirely your fault. Things always had to be your way. You pushed Ripley away. You drove her out into the streets. Now look at her. You were never there for us, always thinking of yourself, always thinking of excursions away. Since Father left, you were so busy with your social life; you forgot we needed you, too. Half the time I was more of a mother to Ripley then you were."

"Are you quite finished with your little verbal attack? I don't have to stand here and listen to this guilt trip you are putting on me." Annalisa's face flushed, knowing deep down there was truth in what she said.

Lauren was like a runaway train, and she had more to say as she pointed her finger in the air. "Yes you do, Mother. It is time you listened—time to quit thinking of just yourself for a change." Her face tightened with each word and she took a deep breath, paused only a moment, and continued her attack. "One of your daughters is lying in there and she may not make it. It's time to be a mother to her for once."

Annalisa spun the ring on her finger around as she tried to defend herself. Prideful, she stood, straightened her posture and shook her head. "Ripley knows how much she means to me."

With an astonished expression, Lauren responded, "Does she?"

It was too difficult to examine any fragments of truth in what Lauren was telling her. All Annalisa heard was the condemning tone in Lauren's voice, and that just made her search for her perspective of the truth. "I've just always found it difficult to express how much I cared. I've done my best. She had everything money could buy. She never lacked anything. If she did need something, all she had to do was ask."

Lauren was determined to say everything she had always wanted to say to her mother. "Yeah, right, she had anything money could buy. That doesn't bring happiness. She never had your love or knew you cared. She was crying out for love and attention her entire life. You were too blind to see it. I was crying out to you too, Mother."

Annalisa just continued to shake her head and tighten her lips as she responded. "Disrespect is all I have ever heard from you or your sister since your dad left."

"Well I've heard it said that respect is something you earn."

"Don't you think I have always wanted the best for you? Many of the things I have done, I have done for both of you. I know it wasn't easy for you living without your father. It was easy for him to move a thousand miles away and start his new life with another woman. Go ahead blame me for everything. Blame me for all your problems, and your bad choices. I'll be your scapegoat, if that is what makes you feel better. That way you never have to look at yourself or blame yourself for your own indiscretions. I know I've made many mistakes over the years. I live with them every day. You were not in my shoes. If you want to judge me, that is your prerogative. I'm not going to listen to any more of this right now. I'm going to see Ripley. When you cool down a little, then we will discuss all these feelings. Take some time to process what you are feeling. I am going to go and be a mother to my other daughter now. Go get yourself a coffee or a glass of wine and calm yourself down."

With a huff, Lauren turned and walked out of the room, shaking her head.

Annalisa stood with a troublesome expression, with condemnation hanging over her head like a lead balloon. Lauren's words had ripped at her heartstrings. She wasn't as cold hearted as some people perceived her to be. Little did they know, her tough disposition was really just her wall of a self-protection to maintain control of her emotions. After all, showing love was a weakness and that would leave her vulnerable to having her heart broken again. As a child, she had been taught to be tough, don't cry, be strong-willed and go after what you want or need.

Here she was waiting, with no control over her daughter's destiny. All her hope was in the hands of the doctors. Thoughts continued to flow through her mind. What does Lauren know about sacrifice? What understanding does she have about my childhood?

She thinks they had it rough. They should try living in a German orphanage like I did when I was a young girl. Huh! Discipline had an entirely different meaning. But I've never ever felt sorry for myself and I'm not going to now! It does seem my children have grown to be as insensitive to my feelings as I have been to their feelings. There is always room for change. Maybe this is the beginning of a new day; a day to make an amends for whatever failures I've made in raising my children. I can only hope that they will be ready or willing to accept that change also. Oh God, I will make things right, if only you heal Ripley and bring her out of this coma. I promise I will be a better mother to them both. I know I've never been much of a religious person. If you are real, then please help my daughters and me.

Annalisa reached over and combed Ripley's hair with her fingers. For the first time, a snapshot moment took place as a compassionate smile fell over her face. Her throat tightened as she patted a tissue around her eyes, holding in her emotions. With her voice shaky and cracking, Annalisa said, "Ripley, when you wake up, I'm going to take you home and I'll make you your favourite soup. Homemade tomato soup with red pepper and onions sautéed in butter, mixed with fresh garden tomatoes and organic cloves of garlic. Just the way you like it, right? I'll take care of you."

Annalisa sat quietly pondering to herself. That must have sounded ridiculous. Even at a time like this I don't know what to say to her. She could be dying and I'm talking about making her soup. I wish my words could tell her how much I love her. I just don't know how to express my love in a language she understands. I have failed her. Lauren is right.

She continued to sit beside Ripley for the rest of the afternoon, until the nurses came in and rolled Ripley onto her other side. The nurse told Ms. Wilks she should go home and get some rest and come back in the morning.

That night was tense for both of them. Annalisa opened the door to the hotel room and threw her coat and purse on the chair. Lauren was sitting on the couch sipping a glass of wine. She reached for the half-empty bottle to fill her glass. "Well, Mother, would you like a glass? It will help you unwind."

Annalisa walked over to Lauren and grabbed the bottle. "You have had enough. You want to talk, then let's talk. I know you blame me for a lot of things that went wrong in our life. Let me tell you that you don't even know the half of it. There are a lot of things you don't know; things that I have kept hidden from both you and Ripley for your own good."

Lauren took a sip of wine to keep her composure, then responded in a clear concise tone, "That doesn't surprise me, Mother. You keeping secrets, that is. My question is, what makes you think that you were protecting us with your secrets? We all know you orchestrated Ripley's abortion. Did you even notice how messed-up that made her? Instead of kicking her out for smoking drugs, did you ever try to understand why she was doing it?"

Annalisa was ready to spew out the truth she had held for such a long time. Lauren's constant badgering released her response. "Do you think I have stupid written on my forehead? Listen to me! I know why she turned to drugs to hide her pain. I know the reason even if Ripley does not know. I know the rapist who attacked her that night. It will do her no good to know who he was."

Lauren almost coughed up her wine. "What are you saying? Who the heck was he? Why was he not charged and put in jail?"

Angry at the entire situation and the turn of events within their lives, Annalisa continued to charge. "Are you really so oblivious that you never figured it out? Do you find it easy to live in denial? You know darn well that it was your father behind that mask. That is why I made her have an abortion, and that is why he left town in such a hurry. I told him to get out of our lives. It was not another woman he was having an affair with. I just made up that story to protect all of us and our reputation. Ripley would be devastated if she knew that it was her father. It doesn't matter anymore. It will remain our secret. Is that clear? Next time you want to bash me and blame me for everything, get your facts straight."

13
A DESPERATE PRAYER

After over a week of talking to police, a criminologist, and a psychiatrist, Roseway had had enough of being in the hospital. Joseph visited her every day when her family wasn't with her. Roseway relished her conversations with Joseph, which brought them even closer together. Before she went back to Kelowna with her family, there was one more thing she wanted to do. She wanted desperately to visit Ripley.

She hadn't forgotten the words spoken to her at that church meeting. As she mulled over the last week, she could hardly believe the turn of events. Reuniting with her family was a miracle. Joseph's persistent determination to find her must have been God's inspiration. His dream and the timing had to be all God's planning. Many of the pieces of the puzzle seemed to fit, except the few pieces which remained missing. Why did Big Joe beat Ripley? How did he survive the fire? How did he find where Roseway was staying, and where was Big Joe now? Just thinking of him hiding in some dark corner shot darts at her mind. *Who is this person who has made my life a living nightmare?* A question heavy on her heart and a prayer she often asked God to reveal. Questions, she had so many questions, yet few answers. Joseph checked with the doctor and asked if he could take Roseway to visit Ripley. They gave their okay.

Roseway stood outside the door with Joseph by her side. "Are you sure you are up to going in there?"

"Yeah, I want to see her so much. I must admit, I feel like it is entirely my fault this happened to her. If I never came into her life, this never would have happened. Big Joe always told me if I ran away he would kill those I love. It looks like he almost succeeded. I want to see her."

Roseway and Joseph hugged each other tight. He spoke gently to her. "You shouldn't blame yourself, Rose. It was not something you had any control over. She will be fine, Rose. I just believe she will be fine." He kissed her on the forehead and ran his fingers down her tiny face. "I'll wait here while you go in and see her."

Joseph went and sat down in a chair and cupped his head in his hands and ran his fingers through his black hair. He began to pray. *Lord God, I pray you will give Rose the strength she needs to be a support to Ripley. Give her your peace and your blessed assurance as she trusts in you. I pray, Lord, that you would bring healing to Ripley and release her from this coma. Let your will be done. Amen.*

Roseway walked into the room and directly to Ripley's bedside. Shocked by Ripley's appearance, Roseway blurted out, "Oh my God."

Seeing Ripley's state brought a rush of panic to Roseway's chest. She looked so vulnerable and helpless lying there.

"What has Big Joe done to you? Oh, Ripley, I'm so sorry." Roseway sobbed uncontrollably as she laid her head on the bed. Roseway said a prayer that reached up into the heavenly realm. The sweet essence of humility and tears flowed like an endless stream. Barely being able to speak, overwhelmed by her emotions, she grunted and groaned words only the Spirit could understand as she travailed for her friend. Then she felt the warmth of a hand patting her head as if to say, "Don't cry." Roseway's sobs stopped as she began to lift her head off the bed rail. Ripley looked at Roseway. A tear trickled from her eye and she whispered Rose's name. Roseway's face lit up with an astonished expression. She burst out with a shout of joy. "You are awake! Oh, thank you, Jesus! Thank you!"

Hearing the commotion, the nurse came rushing into the room. Joseph, Annalisa and Lauren followed behind her. Hearing the door open and people surrounding her, Ripley looked confused. "What is going on? Is it my birthday? Who is having a party? Mother, what are you doing here? Lauren? Rose?" She looked at Joseph. "Who are you?"

"Oh, this is Joseph. Remember I told you about him?"

"I don't remember much of anything. Where am I?"

"You are in the hospital."

Nurse Jenkins interrupted the conversation and told them there would be time for questions and answers later. Everyone must go back to the waiting room so the doctor could examine the patient.

For the next few days, Roseway would sneak out of her room to see Ripley and take her a coffee. Roseway sat on Ripley's bed and they talked and joked with one another. They shared such a strong bond. Roseway tried to lighten Ripley's spirit by painting her nails and combing her hair. Ripley had not regained full use of her right hand, and was feeling a little depressed. The swelling on her brain, accompanied by the coma, caused her some paralysis. Ripley would need some physiotherapy in the following weeks and months to hopefully regain the sensation in her hand. Roseway teased Ripley about the improvement of her facial looks with her new cosmetic nose job and haircut. Annalisa had had the best plastic surgeon come in and fix Ripley's broken nose. She also had a hairstylist come in to fix her hair. The swelling and black eyes were still quite a sight.

14
GOING SEPARATE WAYS

After a couple of weeks had passed, both Roseway and Ripley were given the doctor's okay to go home with their families. Ripley was going home with her mother to recuperate from her broken ribs. She still suffered with the odd headache and would have a therapy nurse come to their home to work on getting the feeling back in her hand.

Roseway signed out of the hospital and asked her family to wait for her while she said her goodbyes to Joseph and Ripley.

Roseway stared into Joseph's brown eyes. His sad-looking eyes gazed right through her. He held her hand and pulled her close. He could feel her heart pounding. As he tried to say his goodbye, it was difficult for him to catch his breath. Words couldn't seem to express the feelings he had toward her. Joseph's heart was breaking at the thought of saying goodbye to her. He felt such a magnetic attraction to her, something deeper than just a physical attraction. It was truly love. It was like they were two branches from the same tree. Under the fluorescent lights her mahogany hair sparkled. He wanted to dive into her hazel brown eyes, hold her in his arms and never let go.

Roseway felt that familiar feeling rise up from within. Her face flushed with desire. She wanted to kiss his lips and run her fingers through his dark hair. She still remembered the pain she had felt from the rejection in the truck. However, the chemistry between them was thick like a potion of love's spell over them. Joseph moved his hand along her arm and put his other hand under her chin. He gently leaned into her and kissed the softness of her lips. The flame of love was like an arrow from an archer's bow directly into their hearts.

Roseway whispered. "I'll take that kiss with me, Joseph. I'll remember it always. I think I love you, Joseph. It is such an incredible feeling I've never felt before. I don't want to say goodbye to you."

His voice was low, soft, and calming. "I know, Rose. I feel the same way about you. We can write each other or phone. I'll drop by and see you when I drive the truck through Kelowna. You'll be going to school, and well...We will see what the sands of time bring. Anyway, you have a lot of catching up to do with your family. I should get on the road now. I have a truckload to pick up. Let's keep in touch. You have my phone number. If you ever need anything, just call me. I'll call you, too, Rose. So long. Keep smiling."

"I can't thank you enough for all you have done for me." She paused, finding it difficult to get her words past her throat. Clutching his shirt in her hands, she pleaded, "Oh, don't go. I can't bear to lose you, Joseph."

He placed his head against hers and kissed her forehead. "You're not losing me, Rose. We will talk. I'll see you again. Be patient; remember, God's timing is perfect."

She stood on the tips of her toes and reached her arms around his strong neck and gave him one last kiss goodbye. Tears flowed from both of their eyes. Like a forever goodbye, they reluctantly let their grip release from each other. Joseph choked out one more "Keep in touch," and waved as he backed out of the hospital doors.

Shoulders slumped, he walked over to his truck, wiped his eyes and drove down the road.

Annalisa wheeled Ripley down to the exit doors where Roseway was still standing. Roseway had just finished wiping her tears. Ripley smiled at Roseway.

"Hey there, my friend, look at you. Your face is all blotchy again. Don't get me crying, too. My face looks bad enough with all this bruising."

"Actually, you are sporting a nice shade of eye shadow. What is it called, black-eyed-blue?"

Holding her ribs, Ripley groaned. "Oh, don't make me laugh."

"Ripley, I feel so bad about what happened to you."

"Rose, don't even mention it again. It was not your doing."

With a hint of hesitation, Roseway awkwardly continued. "I need to ask you some questions. I didn't want to bother you about it when you first woke up. Can you tell me what you remember about what happened to you that night? Can you talk about it? You told me it was Big Joe. How did you know?"

Ripley drifted her mind back in time. "Remember the day when we went to the pool? On the way back to the warehouse I went into the coffee shop to get a coffee from Danny. I accidentally bumped into this guy and made him spill his coffee. I said sorry, but he gave me the dirtiest look. He sent chills down my spine. He was kind of scary looking with a scar on his face. Anyway, Danny gave me a coffee and I came out to you. I saw him staring at us but never mentioned it. I just thought what a freak.

"Well I noticed this guy a couple more times. At first I just thought it was coincidence. When we walked down by the lake that night on the way to the church, I saw him again. Remember when I left you at the Upper Room? He was standing right outside the door. He seemed to duck back so as not to look suspicious.

Then I went to club Cancun, and had a few dances. Sure enough, he was sitting there watching me like a hawk. Man, he made my skin crawl. It was about midnight when I noticed he was gone. I felt relieved. Then he came back in and ordered another drink. I left to go back to the warehouse at one o'clock in the morning. It was such an eerie night. I was just about home. Then all of a sudden this guy comes up from behind me and puts his arms around me and covers my mouth. I'll never forget the rasp in his voice. He asked me what I was doing hanging around his Roseway. He said to me, 'The two of you look like you have developed a nice little friendship. You should not have done that, Ripley. Not so good for you.'

"I asked him how he knew my name. He said, 'I have my way of finding out things. It's nothing personal to you, but I have to teach Roseway a little lesson.' That was when he turned me around and punched me in the ribs. I could hardly breathe from the blow. I fought to catch my breath. Then he continued to talk to me, saying he had been watching us for quite some time. He told me you had tried to kill him and left him for dead. He told me how you hit him over the head and knocked him unconscious. When he awoke, the cabin was on fire and so were his pant legs. He tried to put out the fire on his pants. His legs were burning and in pain. When he put out the fire, he tore off his pants and ran out of the cabin and down to the stream to cool his burns. After that the cabin burned down. He was in such pain that he packed his legs with cold mud from the stream, and then he passed out by the river. For days, the burns on his legs kept him from walking back to the remnant of the cabin.

"He has been searching for you ever since. His search ended when he noticed us together at the coffee shop that day. He rambled something about having to teach his daughter that when he says something, he means it. He said, 'A Father has to have respect from his child. I'm going to take Roseway with me again. She belongs with me.'

"I asked him what his name was. He said, 'Just give Roseway this message from BJ. She will know who I am.'

I blurted back at him, 'You are a psycho. Roseway will never go back with you again. In fact, if the police find out you are here, they will arrest you for kidnapping. They should lock you up and throw away the key.'

"Before I knew it, he hit me again. His fist was in my face. He punched me so hard that I fell backwards and hit my head on the cement. Then I must have blacked out until I heard your voice crying over me. From what he said, I knew he was the Big Joe you had told me about. That is about all I remember until I awoke from the coma, when you were standing by my side."

Roseway looked astonished at Ripley's story—dazed, confused. "He did that to you to punish me? He is my father? No, he is a mad man. He is Satan himself. I hate him with everything I have in me. Big Joe can't be my father."

"Maybe you better talk to your mom and ask her about your father."

"I will ask her, and many other questions. Oh Rip, I bet you are sorry you ever met me. Look at what I've done to you."

"I thought I told you to stop putting a guilt trip on yourself. Don't be silly, Rose. You can't blame yourself. We are the best of friends. I'd take a beating for you any day. But, let me recover from this one first." Ripley held onto her ribs again as she laughed.

"I'm going to miss you so much, Ripley, especially your sick sense of humour. I love you, too, Rip. I've never had a friend like you, not ever. I guess you are going to stay with your mother while you recover? She doesn't seem so bad. Maybe you and your sister will get that new start with your mother. Remember that little talk we had a while back?"

"Yes, Rose, and it looks like you will also get a new start with your family. No turning back now. Time to look forward, right? Hey, if you ever want to share a dumpster with me give me a call."

"I might take you up on that someday, Rip. The time we spent together was short, but it is like we have known each other a lifetime. Forever friends, okay? Let's visit each other on holidays. We can cry on each other's shoulder, and talk about life."

"You've got a deal, pal."

Noreen, Sue and Billy walked over to nudge Roseway along. They had a long drive back to Kelowna. Roseway and Ripley gave each other a long, tight hug until Ripley groaned from the pain in her ribs.

"Oh, sorry, Rip, I didn't mean to hug too tight."

"Don't worry about it."

For Roseway, the day was bittersweet. After dreaming and praying all those years, finally Roseway was on her way home with her mother, sister and brother. It seemed strange. Everyone looked so different from how she remembered. Still, she felt good, getting reacquainted. Through the years, life had made its changes to each of them. Sadness left its void to say goodbye to two people she had grown to love. God had redeemed the time and a divine love poured through her to them and through them to her. Roseway had found love in the midst of her bitterness, resentment, anger and hatred. God shined his light in the darkness. She could see the hope in the future for the very first time. They drove back to Kelowna that day.

15
HOME SWEET HOME

It was a long ride from Prince George to Kelowna. Roseway stared out the window, distracted by many thoughts, flash-backs of so many memories of Joseph, Ripley, and Big Joe. The videotape kept playing in her head. She didn't feel like having much conversation. Her memories were such a part of who she had become. In a strange way she clung to those memories, good and bad. Her introspective thoughts ruled her emotions and her actions toward others.

Just outside of Kelowna, the trees of autumn made a collage of colours along the roadside. Wine vineyards were tucked in amongst the valleys of the surrounding mountains. The mountains surrounded her like a warm, comforting blanket, knowing she was home sweet home. She had a warm fuzzy feeling about coming home, even though the air was cool with the freshness of autumn.

The house seemed smaller than she had remembered, as they drove down the long driveway. Roseway looked around the yard for some familiarity. There stood the old swing set, now aged and rusty. Time had chipped away the paint. The broken chains of childhood hung to the ground. The big slide she once slid down with Billy and Suzie seemed so tiny. The apple trees had grown so lofty, even without any blossoms.

She walked into her home. Sunlight filled the room through the large windows. White cotton curtains floated in the breeze. The wheat-coloured walls made the room warm and inviting. It had that fragrance of home she had long forgotten. There was a familiarity of scents which brought her comfort. Somewhat worn by time, the old flowered couch sat in its rightful spot by the fireplace, just as she had remembered. Momma's bible sat on the coffee table, opened to her favourite Psalm. They hung up their jackets on the coat rack that Billy made in shop class. Billy and Sue sat on the couch, watching Roseway as she walked around the room running her fingers over the walls, and picking up her mother's knick-knacks. She walked over to the curtains and put them up to her face and smelled the fragrance of white linen. Quickly she darted over to the coffee table. Her finger scrolled the page as her eyes read her favourite verse. From one thing to the next, inquisitively she touched everything. Memories played within her mind like the flipping of pages in a scrapbook, one picture after another. Then she sat in the old pine rocking chair that her mother once used to rock her to sleep. The floor squeaked as she rocked, like it had years ago.

She looked over toward Billy and Sue. They patiently waited for Roseway to begin a conversation. Roseway breathed a deep cleansing sigh as she put her hands on each arm of the rocking chair. "Well, I guess I'm home."

Sue responded, "Yes, you are home. It is good to have you back with us. It must feel strange after all these years of being away?"

"Yes Suzie, it is very strange, but also familiar."

Another pause of silence interrupted the conversation from a feeling of awkwardness between them. Billy tried to break the ice with a question. "What kind of things did you do living up in the mountains?"

"I had daily chores I had to do: getting water, milking the cow, hunting and fishing excursions with BJ. Every day we practiced throwing knives. He taught me how to hunt and kill and how to scrape the furs and make things like boots, gloves and coats. I learned of the many herbs and plants that are nutritious to eat."

Sue asked, "What did you do for fun?"

"There was never time for playing or games. BJ was not that playful of a fellow. He always seemed angry. He never talked that much. Just to tell me what I did wrong, which was almost everything I did. That is enough talking about me and him, what about you?"

Sue blurted, "Well, we both snowboard. Billy is on the racing team. He is quite good. Those are his medals hanging there on the wall. As for me, well, I am on the college volleyball team, the baseball team, and I play the guitar and sing."

Noreen brought out some tea in her porcelain tea set along with warmed homemade apple muffins and jam. Roseway sat on the couch and fluffed the pillow beside her, then picked it up and hugged it. She sipped her tea and took a small bite of her muffin. "Hmm, these muffins are so good. I haven't tasted anything this delicious in a long time. Mom, I had forgotten how good of a cook you are."

Noreen stared at her from the rocking chair as she rocked casually back and forth. Billy and Sue finished up their tea and muffins and excused themselves to leave the two of them together. They knew they had some catching up to do. Within the mist of an unfamiliar feeling between them, there was a mother-daughter bond beginning to be restored. They made light conversation while getting reacquainted. Hesitant in discussing BJ, Noreen gently moved the conversation along. "Would you like to tell me a little about the years you lived with Joe?"

Roseway took a deep breath and slowly released the air from her lungs. She fidgeted in her chair, trying to get comfortable. Her hand moved from the arm of the chair to her mouth and she rubbed her knuckles along her lips as if trying to pacify her nervousness while she tried to form a sentence. "I don't know where to start except to say that Big Joe took me away from here. He told me I would never see you, Billy, or Suzie ever again. Constantly he reminded me that if I ever ran away, he would hurt you, even kill you. I believed him. He is a very harsh man. He took me far away to live in this cabin deep in the woods. Mountains surrounded us. There was really nowhere I could run. The only place I could go to was this meadow where wildflowers and grass flourished in the summer months. I felt like I was in God's garden when I went there. Going there was the only place where I could find some solace, sanity and the strength to get through the tough days living with him.

"He did teach me many things about surviving off the land. I had to work hard and do everything he told me to do. If I didn't, I'd get a smack. I hated him so much, yet I had to totally rely on him for everything. Momma, I always hoped someone would come find me and rescue me, but you never came—no one came. I only remember one pleasant memory with him. That was the first time I shot and killed a partridge. He cheered and almost laughed. For a split second he almost seemed human. His reaction surprised me. It was soon lost when he told me to pluck the feathers and disembowel the bird. All these years I never knew he was my father."

Noreen's face took on an expression of panic. "How did you know that he was your father?"

Roseway began to cry, wiping her eyes with the cuff of her sleeve. "Mom, you never ever told me who my dad was. You never told me what happened to him. BJ never told me either. I was always just a little bastard. That is what BJ called me all the time.

If it wasn't for Ripley, I never would have found out the truth. BJ revealed the truth to her, just before he beat her."

Noreen got up out of her rocking chair and walked over and sat beside Roseway and put her arm around her to comfort her. Roseway felt angry with her mother and tried to slide away from her. Noreen pushed forward and slid over with her. "I'm so sorry, honey. I never meant to hurt you. I thought I was protecting you from the truth."

Her mother's arm felt warm and loving. Roseway hardened her heart toward her mother as if to punish her. Her thoughts waged war within her mind. Someone has to be blamed for all that has happened. Why not blame her? After all, she knew about Big Joe and had never mentioned him. She had gotten pregnant by him. Roseway burst out angrily. "Why did he have to be my father?"

Noreen broke like a tamed stallion. "Oh baby, Joe raped me. Then he was never seen again. I never wanted to tell you. You were a little girl. You would not have understood. I had my own difficulty in trying to cope with the emotional upheaval of being raped. I had three children. If it wasn't for my faith and the help Uncle Jim gave, I don't know how I would ever have been free from my past. It has haunted me every day since you have been away. I'm sorry you had to live with him. I'm sorry he treated you so badly. I can only hope that you can forgive me for not being there for you. Lord knows I prayed for you every day. I prayed to God to protect you and bring you home. Now you are home.

"Rose, I'm so thankful God has brought you home. We can't change what has happened or bring back that time that was stolen from us. What we can do is enjoy the time we have now and tomorrow. I believe we will make up for the years lost. We have to take our lives back."

Roseway shut out the invading questions oppressing her mind. Listening to Noreen expressing her heart and emotions, Roseway felt her heart soften like a sponge. She flung her arms open wide and wrapped them around her mother as tightly as she could. They both clung to the embrace, soaking up every bit of love. Tears washed their clothing. Years of time and love lost were redeemed in the quiet of the moment. Time seemed to stand still. They released their warm embrace, blew their noses, and wiped their eyes.

Noreen made them all a nice warm cup of milk before they went off to bed. She tucked her grown daughter into her bed, kissed her on the cheek and said, "Good night, sleep tight, and don't let the bedbugs bite." Noreen realized that her little girl had grown into a young woman. There would always be that need to recapture childhood. After all, she would always be her little girl.

"Mom, I forgive you. I know it wasn't your fault. I love you, Mom. Being home is a dream come true. But Mom, I'm so scared Big Joe will come back. He is out there somewhere and nobody knows where. What if he comes back again?"

"Don't worry; if he comes back, we will be ready. Don't forget, we have God on our side. Don't you lose any more sleep thinking of him! Good night, Rose."

"Night Momma, I love you."

"I love you too, Rose."

16
I am Ripley Wilks

Annalisa wheeled Ripley to the Mercedes parked in front of the hospital doors. Fred the chauffeur helped her into the car. Ripley stared out the window while her mother went on and on about how she would make things better. Ripley's head pounded, and her body still felt weak and sore. Her mother's voice sounded more like chalk on a blackboard rather than bringing comfort. Simply, she wasn't all that interested in anything her mother had to say. She had heard all the promises before. As far as Ripley was concerned, her mother was a selfish, cold, uncaring woman. Ripley was not all that excited about going home. In fact, she would rather live on the street and was planning on leaving as soon as her body healed.

The car pulled up to the exquisite waterfront chalet in the exclusive area of high-end homes in Prince George. Annalisa's husband had been very successful with his investments when they first married. Having a smart business sense, he had bought up businesses that were going bankrupt and turned the companies around. After ten years, he was able to sell the shares for double what he paid. The payoff was huge. When he left, Annalisa made sure she got a big share in the companies. That kept his dirty little secret buried deep under the lies.

The twentieth century home had six bedrooms, four baths, and enough room to house three families. Spectacular views through the three-storey windows often made guests ooh and aah. The spacious kitchen was made for entertaining with its tall ceilings, and granite floors and counters. A warm fieldstone fireplace nestled in the open, wooded, cedar family room. Facing the Fraser River was an extensive stone patio, wicker furniture and an outdoor hot tub. Rock gardens with a wide variety of flowers and mesmerizing groundcover complimented the Hollyhocks. Cheerful sunflowers and hardy, vigorous wisteria were complemented by a splash of zinnia. Plenty of bright foliage enhanced the garden with a variety of coloured leaves; water ponds added a touch of tranquility to the garden.

Cars filled the long driveway like there was an auction sale. Ripley's heart pounded. "What are all these cars doing here?"

Mother cheerfully explained. "It is just a nice welcome home for you, Ripley."

Ripley tightened her lip in protest. "Mother, why did you do this? I just want to go home to bed. I don't want to socialize with all your stuffy friends."

"Oh Ripley, don't be so negative. I thought I was doing something nice for you."

"That is the point, Mother, you never know what it is I want or need."

Lauren's mind was reeling, knowing her mother's secret, and she was also suffering the effects of too much wine the night before. To stop the conversation, she said to Ripley, "Just enjoy the attention. Then you can go up to your room if you want to. For once can we just get along?"

Rolling her eyes, Ripley folded her arms over her sore ribs, curled her lips and grinded her teeth while she stewed in silence. They pulled up to the front of the house, where they helped Ripley out of the car and up the stairs to enter through the front door.

A loud, energetic, "SURPRISE!" roared. Decorations and welcome home balloons filled the room. Annalisa had also arranged catering. Waiters went around serving champagne and finger foods. Everyone quickly forgot Ripley and began to mingle, eat, drink, and be merry. As Ripley sat in the room full of people, her heart sank in sadness. She felt such loneliness within. For a moment she daydreamed about her and Roseway skipping stones across the lake. They really did have a lot of fun together in such a short time. If there was such a thing as a kindred spirit, surely they were it. Ripley missed her friend so much. She missed Jimmy and Jenn, too, wondering what they would be doing back at the old warehouse.

Ripley pondered, looking around at the room full of strangers—that is what they were. They didn't know Ripley, what she thought, wanted or needed. Did they know her favourite colour, or flavour of ice cream? Did anyone know her hopes or dreams? Who could recognize the little girl crying, trapped in a young woman's body? Who were these people? Mere acquaintances, people she had met once or twice in her lifetime. Their plastic smiles and tailored clothing hid their real identities. She thought they were all as phony as the hair dye and make-up they wore. On the surface they all looked like they had life all figured out. Probably deep inside each one of them was a hidden closet full of ghosts. What did it matter, really? Was there anyone who cared enough to try to understand Ripley? Roseway cared, but now she was gone, hundreds of miles away.

Trying to numb her pain, Ripley drank one glass of champagne after another as the night dragged on. No one seemed concerned that she was on medication from the hospital. Lauren noticed her little sis was getting a little too tipsy. She put Ripley's arm around her shoulder and helped her up the stairs to her bedroom. "Why don't you lie down before you fall down?"

"I'll be fine. Don't worry about me," she slurred.

When Lauren left the room and closed the door behind her, Ripley began to cry. She held the pillow close to her breasts like it was a teddy bear. When she closed her eyes, images of Joe punching her in the face flashed back. Old memories of being raped invaded her like a tidal wave sweeping over the shore. Again and again she felt life's suffocating blows drowning her little by little. She put her face into her pillow and screamed as loud as she could so no one else would hear her cry. She punched the pillow, then held her ribs from the pain. Ripley yelled out to her unknown God. She threw the pillow on the floor, sat up and looked at herself in the dresser mirror.

"Where are you, God? Roseway often spoke of you. Where is this peace and love you give to your children? Who am I in this plan you have for life? Am I like a grain of sand on a distant shore? Peril after peril I walk the endless shore, waiting for you to sweep me away with one wave of your hand. As I stare in this mirror, I hate the reflection looking back at me. It is the face of evil laughing at me, a grin like a sneer. He waits with his fowler's snare for me to fall. Where are you, God? I didn't stay with Roseway at the Upper Room. Was that my punishment, to fall into the hands of evil? I'm a cripple now. Who would ever love me?"

Combing her short hair didn't make her feel better about her appearance. The bruises, black eyes and swollen nose left her with a disillusioned perception of herself. Then she listened to the taunting voice inside her head.

Look at your face. You are so ugly. Who will love you now? You look like a monster. No one loves you, neither your mother nor your sister. You just make them angry. Roseway, she even left you. You have no one now. Jim and Jenn have forgotten all about you— out of sight out of mind. Who are you? You are nobody.

She put her hands over her ears. Leave me alone. You are a liar. I don't need anyone. I don't care anymore. The cap on her painkillers popped as she turned the lid and then poured the pills into the palm of her hand.

That's it, Ripley. Take the pills and all your pain will disappear. Take them all. Pouring water into a glass while staring at her reflection in the mirror, she raised the pills up to her mouth and popped a couple, swallowed and washed them down. Take the rest. Do it. Do it. Ripley raised her hand toward her mouth and took a couple more pills and washed them down. Good girl, Ripley, now take the rest, you will sleep like a baby.

Ripley poured the rest of her painkillers into the palm of her hand. Feeling drowsy and a little numbed by it all, she stared at the ugly reflection of herself. The quiet of the room was such a contrast from the noise downstairs. Then she heard a soft whisper from within her mind. This voice was different than the other voice. RIPLEY, MY BELOVED, I AM HERE BESIDE YOU. I WILL NEVER LEAVE NOR FORSAKE YOU. I LOVE YOU. I'VE WAITED A LONG TIME FOR YOU TO CRY OUT TO ME. WILL YOU ALLOW ME INTO YOUR HEART? TURN TO ME AND I WILL DIRECT YOUR PATH. YOU ARE MY CHILD. ALLOW ME TO BE YOUR HEAVENLY FATHER.

Ripley dropped the pills on the floor and staggered over to her bed, feeling drowsy from the pills. She sat on the edge of the bed, then laid down and rolled herself up in a little ball. The room started spinning. The champagne and pills curdled her stomach. She ran to the bathroom and spewed into the toilet. She washed her face with cold water and dried it, then stumbled back to her bed. She closed her eyes to try to stop the spinning. She mumbled lethargically, "I am Ripley Wilks. I am Ripley Wilks. Do you really love me, Lord? Do you really care about me or what I do, where I go?

If you do, Lord, then please show me the way." Ripley drifted into a deep sleep.

17
MY FAMILY

Photographers and television news crews pulled up to the little Kelowna home. A crowd gathered in the driveway, waiting for Ms. Shaffer to bring Roseway out for a little press conference. They were on the morning news. Headlines in the local newspaper read, "Missing Girl Found after Twelve-Year Search." Roseway had become the local celebrity, at least until the next big headline or ski event at the local tourist attraction, the Big White Ski Resort.

All this commotion and attention were making her feel claustrophobic. In a strange way she missed the silence of that meadow and the old cabin. In amongst her bad memories were some good ones, however few. The home she had known for twelve years of her childhood had often seemed like a prison. There was an undeniable connection to Big Joe, the cabin, and its surroundings. Time had etched into her soul something surreal in the mist of her experiences. She missed that quiet place in the meadow, where she could go and pray to God to process her thoughts. The last couple weeks had been such a roller coaster ride. Roseway sat on the couch biting her nails, periodically looking out the window at the remaining press.

Sue stared at her sister, trying to figure out who this celebrity was who had re-entered their home with such turmoil. Awkward silences between them made them strive to communicate and break through that invisible wall. Sue was sensitive to Roseway's uneasiness. Sensing a distance between them, Sue asked Roseway if she wanted to take a bike ride along some trails through the evergreen forest, to get away from all the commotion. Roseway didn't even have to reply, for the sparkle in her eyes lit up and a sneaky grin cracked through the tension on her face.

Roseway followed Sue as they simultaneously bolted out of the room to the garage.

They both ran toward the all-terrain vehicle. Sue threw Roseway a helmet and started the ignition.

"Hurry up and get on."

"You can drive this thing?"

"Yeah, hold on."

The garage door opened and they sped away, spinning rubber onto the paved driveway. Roseway was sitting on the back, holding tight to her sister as they drove past the media. Cameras flashed at them as photographers and television crews rushed toward them. Sue squeezed the throttle to go as fast as the machine would go. A few media cars and vans tried to follow for a while but couldn't keep up to them as they veered off into the forest.

Up and down hills, the trees rushed by as Roseway screamed with excitement. "Yahoo!" Her laughter echoed over the loud engine. Sue drove through a small stream and kept right on going. Water, mud and dirt sprayed up onto their clothing. Roseway was on the ride of her life, better than any amusement park thrill.

Then Sue stopped the ATV and turned around and said, "Okay, now it is your turn to drive."

"What? I don't know how to drive. You must be crazy."

"It's easy. Don't be a chicken."

Sue explained to Roseway about the gas and the clutch. With Sue on the back, Roseway squeezed the gas handle. The engine revved as she pushed in the clutch. The machine jerked into gear. They clutched and jerked along the trail as Roseway became familiar with shifting gears. They laughed and laughed through the trails. The more confident Roseway became at driving, the faster she went. Sue cautioned Roseway to be careful going around corners and to slow it down a little. When they approached a sharp turn Sue was quite familiar with, she yelled, "Slow down! Watch out for—"

It was too late. The four-wheeler spun around the corner as the front tires slid through the mud. They both went flying up into the air and landed in a pool of muddy water. Shocked at being tossed, they sat in the mud, covered from head to toe. They both wiped the mud from their faces.

"Look at what you did now," Sue blurted.

Roseway looked dumbfounded. "I'm sorry. Are you all right?"

Sue threw a handful of mud at Roseway. She threw mud back. They wrestled each other around in the mud until they tired. Then they both looked at each other and said concurrently, "Mom is going to kill us." They laughed until they cried. Arms around each other, they helped each other walk out of the mud pool. Cold and wet, they got back on the muddy vehicle and drove home.

When they pulled into their driveway, most of the media was gone. They dragged themselves into the house, caked in mud. Noreen opened the door and just stared at them. "Where have you two been? What on earth...?"

Sue's face looked blank. "We just went for a ride on the trails."

Noreen tried to hold back from laughing. "Take off those muddy clothes and get yourselves upstairs and get cleaned up. Supper will be ready soon. Don't get mud all over the carpet."

The two girls went up stairs and fought over who would get the first shower.

"You can have the first shower."

"No, you can have the first shower."

Rock, paper, scissors decided the outcome. Roseway undressed and went into the shower. Over the noise from the running water, she shouted, "Hey sis, thanks for taking me for a ride today. That was a riot. I really needed that. You are a really cool sister."

"Glad to have you back, Rose. We have a lot of catching up to do."

Like two new pennies they walked down the stairs together. With shiny noses and bright smiles they sat at the kitchen table.

Smelling the aroma of the food, Roseway asked, "What is for dinner? It smells delicious."

Sue reminded Roseway that it was their annual Sunday night dinner. It made their mouths water with anticipation. "It is roast beef, mashed potatoes and turnip for supper and Mom's yummy apple pie for dessert."

Noreen confirmed, "Yes it is. Now, how about you girls set the table while I cut the roast and make gravy?"

Billy came through the door. "Boy, I'm hungry. What's for dinner?"

They sat down, gave thanks to the Lord then began to dish out the food. A startling ring rang out from the phone.

Billy asked, "Should I get it?"

Noreen replied, "It's probably media again. I'll answer the phone."

She lifted the receiver to her ear and said hello. First there was silence, then eerie breathing hung on the other end. There was an abrupt click followed by a buzz and a loud dial tone. Noreen grimaced as she felt her blood pressure rise up to flush her face. She swallowed the tightness in her throat, then walked back to the dinner table, face flushed and clammy.

"Who was on the phone, Mom? You look like you saw a ghost."

"Oh, it was nobody. Wrong number, I guess?" Anxiously, Noreen changed the subject by asking the girls about their adventurous ride.

After dinner, Billy lit the fireplace, Roseway made hot chocolate and Susie put together a plate of cookies. The smell of the fire and the warmth made their little family game of Scrabble cozy. Noreen lit a few scented candles around the room for a little more ambience. They all snuggled around the table.

"Hey Rose, maybe playing Scrabble will improve your spelling?" Susie teased.

Roseway blurted back, "Yeah and maybe a game of Scrabble will unscramble your brain."

They laughed and joked. Realizing how great it was to have the family back together, Noreen couldn't help but smile with joy. It was a moment she had dreamed about for years. After the game, they went up to their rooms for the night.

Noreen stayed downstairs and locked up all the doors. The phone call earlier in the evening still gave her an uneasy feeling in the pit of her stomach. When she was sure everyone else was upstairs and in their rooms, she quietly took her rifle out of the cabinet and loaded it. It could drop a moose at a hundred yards. She took it up to her room with her. For a while she sat in her rocking chair looking out of her bedroom window. With the gun on her lap she rubbed its barrel, making it shine. The moon was full and the sky was clear. The stars shined like diamonds on a black velvet cloth. She prayed as she rocked quietly back and forth. The Lord is my refuge and my strength. You are my hiding place. In you, Lord,

I put my trust. Please protect my children from the hands of evil. Equip me also to do what I must do, to protect them. I won't allow that man to hurt my family again. She nodded off to sleep with the gun resting on her lap and her finger near the trigger.

18
THE DUMPSTER CALLED DENIAL

It was eleven o'clock in the morning. Lauren pounded on Ripley's bedroom door. "Sleepy head, wake up. You already missed breakfast and you will miss lunch, too, if you don't get your butt out of bed. It is time to do your physiotherapy." Lauren opened the door and walked over to Ripley. She picked up a pillow off the floor and threw it at her. "Hey sleepy head, get up." Ripley didn't move. Lauren noticed the spilled bottle of pills on the floor. Then she yelled, "Mother! Get a doctor quick. Ripley is unconscious."

Lauren gently tapped Ripley on her face, then harder as panic festered. "Wake up, wake up."

Ripley awoke. "What the...? What do you think you are doing? That hurt, you moron."

"Ripley, you scared the hell out of me. I thought you ..."

"No, I was just having a nice dream until you came in yelling and slapping me around. I'm just a little tired this morning, and do I ever have a headache."

"You had too much champagne last night. What are these pills doing all over?"

"Oh whatever...Could you just leave me alone? I don't feel like getting up yet."

"I'll go get you a cup of coffee while you get yourself together. I'm not going to allow you to sleep the day away. The physiotherapist will be here at one o'clock. We have to get that hand of yours back to proper working order."

Over the next several months, Ripley met her physiotherapist for regular appointments. The progress was amazing, as she regained most of the feeling in her fingers. Her face was back to its beautiful features. Now and then the pain of migraine headaches almost made her pass out. She had even enrolled in her first semester in psychology and social work, loving every minute of it. It helped getting out of the house and away from Mother. However, their relationship was changing for the better. Lauren had moved back to her apartment when she saw Ripley had improved physically.

Professor J.D. Cleveland was Ripley's psychology teacher. He was young and fresh, a graduate out of university with his diploma in-hand. This was his first year taking on the teacher's role. J.D.—John David—Cleveland grew up as a farm boy in Saskatchewan. Combining fields of wheat all day was not quite stimulating enough for J.D.'s overactive mind. When he was eighteen, he couldn't leave the farm soon enough to pursue a degree in psychology. After seven years studying at the University of Waterloo, here he was, twenty five years old, quite eager to share his wealth of knowledge with the new roster of eager students. Professor J.D's teaching skills were put to the test the very first class by this feisty young student named Ripley Wilks. J.D. knew right away he was in for a challenge.

Ripley was a determined new student, eager to achieve high grades. She had her own stubborn views, which tested the professor day after day as she spoke confidently in class debates. J.D. found Ripley's challenging questions intriguing to say the least. After class, Ripley often lingered by his desk prodding a little deeper to continue the class discussions. The little one-on-one teaching after class also improved Ripley's understanding of all the insecurities she held within. In her classes they studied the causes of fear and the reactions to fear. Other topics explored dealt with other emotions like anger, bitterness, and rage. These studies gave Ripley a lot of insight into her own emotions and some of the hostility she felt toward her mother.

One day after a class discussion on emotional healing, Ripley engaged the professor in one of her further cross-examinations. Being the last student in the classroom, Ripley leaned against his desk and dropped her assignment into his lap. The topic of discussion was about denial, cognitive dissonance, defence mechanisms, and self-protection. Ripley felt comfortable talking with Professor J.D. Before she knew it, she was spilling her story over the pages of his desk.

"Professor J.D., I found our class discussion interesting. I could relate to the topics. For years I always tried to erase any traumatic events from my mind, not deny they happened, but deny any good reason to deal with my feelings. It seemed easier to run away from home and, in essence, run away from my hurt, pain and anger. In doing so, I chose to live in the dumpster called denial. Did you know that I lived on the street for about a year? In actuality, I was finding the good things in the dumpster to survive while leaving the rest of the garbage in the dumpster.

"I can kind of parallel what became a reality of living for me, to the scenario discussed in class about the dumpster of denial. Sometimes leaving that garbage in that dumpster seemed like the only way to cope, if you know what I mean? You know, don't face the fear, but instead flee from it.

"Eventually, the ride had to stop. That is when I had to face the fact that yes, I was raped. A part of me felt like I had died in that moment. It was a violation of something so intimate. That man stole my innocence, my childhood when he raped me. Next thing I knew, I was pregnant. My mother convinced me to have an abortion by leading me to believe that it was the best thing to do. I went through with it, but I always hated her for it. It was like we had to hide our filthy family secret. In doing so, I had to hide away my feelings in the process. Deep down, I blamed my mother for everything that ever went wrong in my life.

"Then there were the emotions of self I never realized existed. I think the hardest thing to overcome is in taking responsibility for our actions or lack of response even. I realized that as much as I was angry at my mother, I was angry at myself for allowing myself to get into a position that caused such negative things to occur. I would project or displace all of my feelings. Somehow, I had given over the control of my life to circumstance.

"When I lived on the street, that was when I truly believed I was at the least the one in control of my life. There were no rules or expectations to live up to. It felt freeing. It wasn't until I was beaten up and almost lost my life that I also realized there are always consequences. Things happen beyond our control. The first step in my healing was in admitting my own weaknesses. When I began to do that, I was angry at myself. I didn't like myself for not speaking up or being strong enough to make a choice to have that baby. Having the abortion not only killed that baby, it killed what was left of me. I lost my identity in all of it. Now that I am dealing with my anger, the regret and the pain of my past, my perspective about many things is changing. Definitely my anger has subdued. Or maybe I have learned to channel it into a positive direction? What do you think, Professor?"

"Well, Ripley, you just mentioned about half a dozen topics we could discuss. I'm not a counsellor, but have studied to some extent emotional healing. In brief it sounds like you have done a lot of thinking about your life and those traumatic experiences. Whenever you can find a positive perspective, that is always a good beginning. Our future class discussions will touch on some of these scenarios."

"Well professor, would you like to go for a coffee and continue our conversation? I'd be very interested in hearing what you have to say."

"That would be nice, Ripley, but that is not in keeping with the teacher-student protocol. Feel free to visit me during my office hours."

"Oh professor, I just wanted to pick your brain a little, not go to bed with you."

He raised his one eyebrow as his face blushed, and he tried to change the topic. "Well, I better get going. I have all these assignments to mark. We will have that conversation at a more appropriate time and place."

As Ripley walked gracefully toward the door, she turned her head and said with a smile, "I'll see you at class, Professor Cleveland."

Professor Cleveland said in a low tone, "Next class then, Ripley."

When she closed the door, he wiped the sweat from his forehead, thinking to himself, Wow, very intriguing. Definitely has my attention. I better be careful with this one.

As time went by, it was becoming more and more difficult to conceal the attraction between them. Subtle flirtations with one another also increased. There was a definite chemistry between Ripley and the professor. Professor J.D. was not about to cross the teacher-student rules, even though his emotions battled for control every time he was near Ripley.

Both Ripley and Roseway were quite involved in their school studies. Their relationships with their families were reconciling in many ways. In their spare time, they wrote each other letters. They checked their mailboxes frequently, anxious to connect. They really missed each other. Roseway didn't have Internet, so early on it was decided they would both use snail mail. The time between letters made each one that much more urgent. After ripping the envelope open, Roseway would take her letter and go sit by the fireplace, pull a soft blanket over her legs, cozy herself, and read and examine every word. It took time, but Roseway would pronounce out each word and read the letter over and over again.

Dear Rose,

How are you adjusting to being home? I guess the press has stopped hounding you now? Things are looking up around here. I just started my first semester at the University. After looking through some magazines, I realized that I wanted to make a difference in other people's lives. Help others with the same things I have struggled with. Now here I am, taking psychology classes. Can you imagine that? I find it very interesting, and I am gaining understanding to how some people tick. My Prof. is so nice, very attractive too. I think I might be falling for him. But he doesn't date students. After class I make a point of staying behind to talk to him. Sometimes we have long discussions. We think the same way about many things. We have similar interests and dreams in regards to our futures. Why, we practically end each other's sentences. He likes French vanilla cappuccino, wears Calvin Klein jeans and Escape Cologne. He smells delicious. I think he is part of my new inspiration to succeed. I can't wait to finish this course; maybe then he will date me and get over that wall of rules. Hey, you know me, never been much for obeying rules. Perhaps this is a lesson in patience that God is teaching me?

I hope you didn't fall off your chair reading that last sentence. You heard me correctly. I did mention God. I'm going to church now, big surprise, eh? After you left Prince George, things just seemed to close in on me. One night I was ready to end it all. I had the pills in hand, even swallowed a few. I started to enter that dark tunnel called despair. It was pulling me in. Just before I was about to finish the bottle of pills, I heard this very different voice speak to me. It wasn't really an audible voice. It was just this peaceful voice inside my head. It was different from the negative voice which kept telling me how useless and unloved I was. No, this voice was loving and clear. It astonished me. At first I thought the pills were making me delusional. It seemed very real to me. That night, I became a believer. I've been seeking God's guidance ever since. It is still not easy sometimes. I understand a little better now the struggle you often felt between good and evil. I'm learning that the first step in any healing is coming out of that denial and entering into acceptance and admitting when we do have a problem. Anyway, things are good.

You should see my nose. Since the surgery, my nose looks better than it did before. My ribs are healed. I almost have all the feeling back in my hand. It is just difficult to pick up small items, and playing the piano is tough. Hey, it gives me an excuse for playing the wrong keys. I miss you, Rose, and can't wait to see you again. I'll see you during the Christmas break. Keep in touch. I love you, Rose.

BFF,

Ripley

Enthusiastic, Roseway would reply immediately after studying Ripley's letter. Her spelling was improving. She had a strong determination to learn. Noreen would spend time helping her. They would sit on the couch and read books together as if Roseway was still Noreen's little girl. There were so many childhood things that they both missed out on doing together. Whenever they could, they did things together to capture as much mother-daughter time as possible.

Roseway was old enough that she still wanted her privacy and liked to keep her letters to and from Ripley like they were her own prize possessions. She kept each letter in a little treasure box she wove from pine needles. Regardless of spelling mistakes and errors, she mailed her letters off. These letters were therapeutic in their own way. With Ripley, Roseway felt she could share anything. They had no secrets, no false perception about each other.

Dear Ripley:

Hey Pal, it was so good to here from you. I can't wait until Christmas to see you again. I am in shock at the news. Sounds like you have a major crush on your Profesor. Or is it love...? I'm hapy for you. You are going to church now. That is a switch. I hope things are a little beter betwen you and your Mother.

It was a big ajustment coming back home after being away so long. It was like we all had to get to know each other all over again. Suzie and I have been really bonding, catching up on sister stuff. She is fun to hang out with. I'm getting some scooling myself. Not getting a B.A or anything like that, but maybe some day. My spelling is improoving. I hope you noticed.

Billy is always out, usually snowboarding at Big White and going in competitions. I even tried snow boarding once, almost killed myself when I wiped out—almost hit a tree.

Joseph is stopping by for a visit next week. He has a delivry to make in Kelowna. He might spend the night. Mom says he can sleep on the couch. I really have strong feelings for him. My palms swet and my face gets flushed when he calls. Mom is always smiling. I sense the hapiness she is feeling having me home. Other times, when she thinks we don't see her, she looks worried. Some times the phone rings, and then there is no one on the other end when we pick up. It is freaky. Don't worry though, I dout that Big Joe will come back here again. That is enough about that crap. I'll be waiting to see you at New Years. We will catch up then.

BFF, Love Roseway

19
CHRISTMAS

Ripley and Roseway had planned on a New Year's reunion for the past few months. It was now two days after Christmas. Ripley had enjoyed having Christmas with her mother, Lauren and her new boyfriend, Bob. Ripley invited her friends Jenn and Jim to join them for dinner. This Christmas was much different from the previous Christmases, when Mother would invite all her friends to an evening of drinking, dancing, a smorgasbord of food and presents galore. This year it was a quiet dinner for six. Jim played the guitar as they all joined in singing Christmas carols.

Jim shared the good news that he had acquired a job playing his guitar and singing at a night club. He was making really good coin and was quite happy to say that he'd even found a cheap room where he could stay. After the incident with Ripley and Joe, the police forced him and Jenn out of the warehouse. The next month, the warehouse was demolished. That was when Jim started searching for someplace else to live. The club owner, Sketch Owens, liked Jim. Jim impressed him when he auditioned. So much so that he gave him a job and a room.

Jenn was staying at a woman's rehabilitation shelter. It was too cold to be out on the street. She was trying to kick her drug habit. She said she was in the middle of a program that was training her to learn the necessary skills so she could go out and get a job and eventually become self-sufficient. She was also volunteering to speak to other young girls in the schools, as a way of taking preventive action for teens thinking about leaving home. There was a change in Jenn's disposition. Ripley and Jim noticed it right away.

Here they were at Christmas, their lives totally changed in positive ways. They were all going in new directions. The smiles on each of their faces lit up the room as much as the candles. They sang songs until midnight. Ms. Wilks gave both Jenn and Jim cards with cheques enclosed. She thought it might help them get back on their feet. When they opened their cards, their mouths dropped open in shock, humbled by the gift. It was a wonderful Christmas Eve together. Jim and Jenn left together, around midnight. Ripley commented on what a nice couple the two of them would make. She couldn't help but notice the way they eyed each other all day. They all said their Christmas cheers and good wishes.

The house quieted as it emptied. Calming Christmas carols played in the background. Ripley and Lauren sat down by the Christmas tree with their mother, Annalisa. It was their German tradition to open their gifts on Christmas Eve. Annalisa brought out two nicely wrapped boxes. Then she began to talk a little about the gifts.

"I just want to say that I am thankful that both my daughters are here this Christmas. I know that I have made my share of mistakes in raising both of you. I'm sorry for those mistakes. I hope that the future will be better. I believe it is never too late to change things. That is why this Christmas I'm trying to do things a little differently. I only have this one little gift for each of you. I didn't buy them. They have a great sentimental value for me. I have kept them all these years hidden in a box. Go ahead, you can open them."

Ripley and Lauren both began to remove the paper from their gifts. Ripley tore the paper from her gift first, while Lauren was still admiring the beautiful wrapping on hers. When she removed the paper, Ripley held a little box in her hand. Embroidered flowers covered the fabric on the box. Delicately, Ripley lifted the lid. Inside was a necklace with a heart locket. She opened the locket and inside was an old black and white picture, stained yellow from the years. On one side was a man and on the other a woman. Eyes watering, Annalisa watched Ripley's inquisitive expression as she explained that the picture was of Oma and Opa. Never before had Annalisa ever spoke a word to Ripley or Lauren about the story of her childhood. Holding back her tears, her voice quivered as she began to tell them about the locket. In a German dialect she said, "This locket belonged to Oma."

"Speak English, Mother," the girls both blurted out.

"Well, as I was saying, the picture was taken of them on their wedding day. It was during World War II. My Papa was working outside with the farm animals. My Mutti was baking bread and cooking homemade soup. I was about six years old at the time. Mutti sent me out to get Papa to come in for lunch. I remember the day so clearly. The sun was shining and you could hear the thunder of the bombs in the distance. Papa always said not to worry and that the German army would protect us. I went out and told Papa dinner was ready.

"It was about three o'clock in the afternoon. Before Papa went in the house to wash up, he told me to close the gate for the chickens and then come into the house. When I was doing that chore, the ground started to shake under my feet. It was like a mini earthquake. When I looked, I could see dust on top of the hill, just a little to the south of our farm. Out of this dust bowl came a big army tank. It shot bombs from its long canon directed at our house. The house exploded in front of my eyes. Debris went flying everywhere. I ducked down and hid under a wooden storage box. I remember yelling, "Mutti, Papa!" Then another bomb hit what remained of the house.

"The force of the bomb must have knocked me out for a few minutes. When I awoke, there were soldiers taking our chicken eggs. Some of the soldiers were taking milk from the cows; pulling the cows udders, filling the bucket and playfully having milk fights in-between pulls. I remained still as if I were dead, for fear that they would kill me, too. When they left, I got up and tried to find my parents. I found them dead. There was not much else to find in the rubble. I found my mother's locket in one of these two boxes. One had some jewellery and the other some of my papa's keepsakes— some cufflinks, and an old medal of honour that belonged to my grandpa from World War I. Somehow I survived. They were the few things I retrieved from our home, before the German soldiers found me.

"That was when they put me in an orphanage. In the orphanage, they trained us to work hard and prepared us for battle. We were treated like little soldiers, girls or boys, it didn't matter. It was very strict training. There was no love or compassion. I kept this locket all these years and the gift in Lauren's box, too. I want you to have them."

Lauren opened her gift box. The box still had some burn marks on it from the bombing. From inside the box she pulled out a gold bracelet with engraving on it: "Forever love." Lauren and Ripley looked at each other, then at their mother. Ripley thanked her mother and went over to her and hugged her.

"Mother, this is the most heartfelt gift. It must have been difficult for you to give these to us. I'll cherish it always. Thank you."

Lauren paled, remembering the words she had spoken to her mother months back. "Mother, I don't know what to say. Thank you. I had no idea...I . . ."

"It's okay, dear. I know. You are both welcome." She hugged Lauren, too. "Enough of this mushy stuff," she said, trying to break the awkwardness of the moment. "There is one other thing I was thinking, and that is that maybe the three of us could go on a trip together, to some nice warm beach in the islands, maybe between your school semesters? We have never done a trip together. What do you think about that idea?"

Smiles lit up their faces. Excited by the idea, Ripley responded. "Yes, that sounds like a wonderful idea. Count me in. Could we bring Roseway, too?"

"I don't see why not. What do you think, Lauren?"

"That is a great idea. Sounds like a lot of fun. Count me in, too."

"We have a gift for you too, Mother," Ripley said.

It was an enlarged picture of the three of them, framed and matted. Annalisa smiled as she looked at the picture. There was a look of pride in her eyes. "My girls," she said softly.

Ripley was impressed with the change she was witnessing in her mother. She had not noticed this generous side of her before, at least not until now. Ripley had always perceived her mother's giving as being more like a pacifier, a means to keep them out of her hair. Surprisingly, Ripley was starting to see her mother in such a different light. At the same time, Annalisa was appreciating having Ripley home. The two had really bonded since Ripley moved back home. They were really getting to know each other.

* * *

Roseway and her family had their traditional Christmas. They all gathered with the neighbours for a horse-pulled sleigh ride, sipped hot chocolate and sang carols around the outdoor fire. After they retired to the house, where Momma lit all her candles and then read the Christmas story. Suzie played Silent Night and Away in the Manger on her guitar.

At midnight, they were each allowed to open one Christmas present. Roseway had made her brother Billy a pair of leather gloves and for her sister Suzie a leather guitar strap. She gave Noreen a basket she wove out of pine needles. She had filled the basket with herbs and spices.

Noreen gave Roseway a beautiful journal book with a scripture verse at the top of each page. The front cover had a picture of a sheep which had fallen over the ledge of a cliff, but landed on a ledge below. Above the sheep stood a shepherd holding his staff and bending down to rescue the sheep.

20
A GIFT OF LOVE

It was two days after Christmas. Ripley rushed around the house like a kid excited to visit Disneyland. She packed her suitcase and wrapped the Christmas present she bought for Roseway. It was at least a ten-hour drive from Prince George to Kelowna and she wanted to get there as soon as she could. She made herself a couple of sandwiches and a thermos of coffee.

"Mother, I'm heading out to drive to Kelowna now."

Mother poked her head around the kitchen door and yelled, "Wait a minute!" Then she made her way over to Ripley and gave her a hug. "Careful on the roads and call me when you get there. I love you."

Ripley paused for a moment, almost surprised at her mother's display of affection, then responded with a hug. "I love you too, Mother."

Ripley drove through the mountains at a steady pace, only stopping once for a bite to eat. It was about ten-thirty at night when she pulled into the long driveway of 572 King Street. The Christmas lights were on. She could see the decorated tree through the big double-pane window. The black sky and bright stars reflected through the window onto Roseway's smiling face as she peered through the curtain-drawn window. Within seconds she came rushing out of the door, face gleaming and arms open wide.

"I'm so glad you are here. Come on in; let me help you with your things. Momma has the kettle on and her homemade pie is warm. She just took it out of the oven."

After some warm-hearted conversation over coffee and dessert, Roseway took Ripley up to her bedroom. It was getting quite late and Ripley was tired from the long drive. As they unpacked her suitcase, they caught up on all the events of the past couple of months. Roseway was full of excitement and talked continuously as Ripley listened.

"So Rip, tell me more about your professor. From what you said in your letter, it sounds like you are quite smitten with him."

"Yes, I think he is very handsome. He also has a great mind. His class has helped me to see things with an open perspective. Also, I think that he is attracted to me. He has that look in his eyes when he looks at me."

"I know what you mean. Joseph looks at me with these puppy love eyes. We call each other every day. When he was here Christmas day, I didn't want him to leave. I can't believe that my life has changed so much in the last two years. God really did answer my prayers. At the time it seemed like God didn't even hear me. Now when I look back, I can see that God was answering my prayers, but in his time not mine. It's amazing, and now you are going to church, too. What a change your life has taken. Tell me about your life-changing experience?"

"There really isn't much to tell. I was in a real state of depression when I returned home from the hospital. I wasn't thinking straight. It just felt like this dark cloud was hanging over me. It almost felt like it was smothering me. I didn't like myself one little bit when I looked at myself in the mirror. I felt like ending it all. I was a little drunk and I took some pills. I felt desperate and really very lonely, even though the house was full of people.

"I guess it was in my state of desperation that I cried and yelled out to God. I was about to take the rest of the pills and then peace came over me, and it was like I heard an inaudible voice speak to me. It was kind of like a father speaks to a child. This voice was different from the other voice that seemed to taunt me. Then I dropped the pills on the floor. I just knew that something had changed. In that moment I had changed. When I awoke the next morning, the depression was gone, and other than the splitting headache I had, life seemed much more liveable. I even went to a church that following Sunday."

"That is so fantastic, Ripley. Things are so great and I'm so happy. Getting to know my family again has been wonderful. I'm kind of afraid, though. Things just seem too perfect. I wonder when the next valley will come. Will I wake up one day and find out that this is all just a dream, and in reality I'm still trapped in that cabin with Big Joe? What do you think?"

Roseway looked over at Ripley after putting her last shirt from her suitcase into the dresser. Ripley had fallen asleep. Roseway smiled, and covered her with a blanket. Roseway turned off the light and went to bed. She whispered, "Goodnight, my friend."

The house was quiet with everyone asleep. The night stars and moonlight shone through the window. Billy's snore moved through the thin walls.

Louder still was the sound of a loud crash coming from the outside of the house. It made the walls shake and awoke the entire household. Awakening from their deep sleep, they all sat up out of their beds and then ran toward their bedroom doors. Noreen came running down the hallway with rifle in hand yelling their names,

"Rose, Billy, Sue!" The four of them were standing at the top of the landing.

"Stay together and don't move." Noreen yelled as she made her way to them.

"What was that noise, Momma?" Sue asked.

"Shh...everyone keep quiet and stay behind me."

Huddled close to each other, they followed Noreen down the stairs. Each floorboard creaked in the silence as their hearts pounded with trepidation. Billy let out a loud fart. Rose, following behind him, gave him a punch in the arm. "You stink." Roseway was getting a little perturbed at the situation. She noticed the gun quivering in her momma's hands.

Roseway said to her mother, "Give me that gun. I know how to use it."

Before Noreen could respond, Roseway yanked the gun from her hand and flipped on light switches as she made her way down the stairs. Noreen ran to the phone and dialled 911. Roseway opened the front door and walked in the direction of the noise. As Roseway started to go out the door, Ripley yelled to her, "Stay in the house and wait for the police to get here."

Rose's determination ignored Ripley's instruction. Even though she felt fearful, her protective love for her family and friend was more powerful. She looked around in the darkness, noticing the front windshield of Ripley's car had been smashed. A large rock had been thrown through the windshield and lay on the car's front seat. It had a piece of paper taped to it. Roseway reached inside the car and pulled off the paper. It read, "Happy New Year." She heard a noise rustle in the bush behind her and spun around pointing the gun.

"Come out of there now, you coward. We are not afraid of you. The police are on their way. Leave us alone, BJ, or I'll kill you."

She sounded quite brave, but her heart was pounding with fear. Seconds later the sound of sirens matched the red lights driving along Mountain Road.

The police arrived and did a thorough search around the property, but found nothing. They questioned each of them. Noreen asked if the police could provide them with round the clock protection. The officer said that they would keep a patrol car out front for the rest of the night, but that tomorrow they could only do periodic patrols. They had a profile picture of Joe and said they would be on the lookout for anyone resembling the sketched photo that Roseway had already given to the police.

After all of the excitement, things started to settle down. Noreen told them they should all get to bed and try to get some sleep. Everything would be fine with the police parked out front of the house. They made their way to bed, all talking to each other through the bedroom walls until sleep claimed them.

Sunrise came quickly, and one by one they all made their way down the stairs to the kitchen. The smell of apple pancakes, smoked bacon and freshly brewed coffee called them to breakfast. Billy and Sue were the first to the table. They both had to catch the bus shuttle to Big White in time to go in the snowboard competition. While eating the first helping of pancakes, they rehashed the last night's events.

Billy commented, "Wow! That was totally rad last night. Did you see Rose? Man she was pumped. I bet if that dude Joe was out there, she would have shot him down."

Sue was less enthusiastic. "I don't think that Rose should have run out of the house so recklessly. That Joe sounds like a bad dude."

"Maybe so, but he would have been a dead dude if Rose saw him."

Noreen tried to end the conversation by hurrying them to get ready to catch the bus. Ripley meandered around the corner, fluffing her blonde hair as she headed for the coffee pot.

"Morning," she said groggily. "I could smell the coffee from upstairs."

Roseway was next around the corner. "Hey, could you poor me a cup while you are at it? I've kind of acquired a taste for that stuff. Could you put in four sugars and lots of cream?"

Ripley poured an extra cup and left it sitting on the counter, then went to sit at the table.

"Would you like a couple of pancakes, Ripley?" Noreen asked.

"No thanks. I'm not hungry this morning."

Fixing her own coffee, Roseway piped up. "Oh come on, Rip. You need to eat something."

"Really, if I wanted something to eat, I would have said yes."

"Well, I just thought—"

"That's a first," Ripley said, interrupting her.

"What are you talking about?"

"Well, if you had of used your brain last night instead of running out of the house half cocked, that would have been thinking."

"What flew up your nose this morning?"

"You did."

"Everything turned out fine last night. Whoever was out there last night is gone."

"Fine? You think everything is fine? My mother's car has no windshield left. There is a Happy New Year boulder sitting on the front seat of my car. Some psycho, probably Joe, is stalking us and you think everything is fine? What are you smoking?"

"Ripley, I think you need to get a grip on yourself."

"Oh is that right? You just don't get it, do you? Joe is crazy. That man almost killed me. I remember well the evil in his eyes." Hands shaking, she took a sip of her coffee. "You think running out in the dark last night with that gun was a smart thing to do? What were you thinking? Did you want to be the big brave hero? Don't you know that most times heroes end up dead? That was the stupidest thing I've seen you do. He could have killed you."

"He is not going to kill me. I understand him. After all I lived with the man for many years. For years I was afraid of him. For the first time, I'm not afraid of him anymore. Well, maybe a little. Last night I faced my fear. It felt good, actually. Now he is gone, hopefully forever."

"Yeah and what happens when he comes back? Are you going to be everyone's big protector? You and what army? I don't mind saying that I am really scared right now. I still have nightmares of him. Not only that, now I have to get my mother's car fixed. You think it is all a big joke."

"That is not true!" Feeling overwhelmed by the intense conversation and Ripley's harsh tone, Roseway left the kitchen as her eyes started to well up with tears. She ran up the stairs.

Noreen and Ripley looked at each other. Noreen wanted to run upstairs after her. Ripley tightened her mouth and sighed loudly. "I'm sorry, Ms Shaffer. Maybe I was a little harsh. I'll go talk to her. I have a bad feeling when I think of that guy. He has caused enough trouble. Why can't the police catch him and lock him away forever?"

Roseway jumped onto her bed and put her face in the pillow and let out a muffled cry as she started talking to the Lord.

"Father God, what has just happened? Why is Ripley being so harsh toward me? I thought I was doing the right thing last night. You told me, I need to face my fears and that is what I did. Lord I do pray that you would take Joe away forever. Keep him from tormenting my family and my friend. If only the police would catch him, and then maybe he could get some help."

Ripley came up to the bedroom to see if Rose was all right. As she stood outside the bedroom door, she heard Rose praying and didn't want to interrupt, so she waited and listened.

"I also want to pray for Ripley that you heal those emotional scars; in the same way that you have been healing mine. Lord God, please protect her and my family from Joe. Ripley is the best friend I have ever had and I wouldn't want to hurt her for the world. Please Lord, help us this day to face our fears. Thank you, Lord, for the answers to prayer you have given. It brings comfort and strength to know you are near. Lord, be my confidence, I pray. Amen."

Roseway felt a hand on her shoulder as Ripley kneeled down beside and placed her hand over Rose's. When Roseway finished praying, Ripley began to pray.

"Lord, you know I'm not much good at praying, but I pray for Rose and for Noreen, Billy and Sue—that you would give them a life, free from this man Joe. He has taken so much from them already. I pray you will help the police to find Joe soon. Thank you for bringing Rose into my life. Jesus, please be with us throughout this day. Amen!

"Rose, I'm sorry I was so hard on you down stairs. I am just very tired, edgy and scared."

Hugging Ripley, Roseway replied, "That is okay. I understand your uneasiness. Everything will be fine. I just know it will. Hey, I got you a little something for Christmas. It is not much, but I made it for you. Do you want to open it now?" Roseway handed Ripley an awkwardly wrapped present with a little card attached. "You have to read the card first."

Ripley took the card out of the manila envelope. The card had a picture with two little girls on the front. They both had watering cans and were watering a garden of flowers. They both wore little bonnets. One little girl was wearing a blue dress and the other was wearing a yellow dress. When Ripley opened the card, she began to read Rose's hand-written poem.

Dear Ripley,

I pray you have the Best Year Ever. May this poem always be an encouragement to you. I pray that God will bless you in everything that you do. Always seek to find the good in all circumstances. Things are not always as they appear on the surface. It may seem like a silly gift, but I think it says so much more.

Love, Roseway

Artistry
God's artistry is an amazing design.
Should wonder ever cease?
The valleys are filled with silent peace.
Everything has a unique form or shape.
In a blink of an eye the clouds cover the earth like a cape.
A person can seem cold and rough.
Because of a life once controlled by sinful stuff.
Within a twinkle of the eye,
God's hand can come down from the sky.
Mould and shape what may seem ugly and trite.
Turn it into a beautiful sight.
If what you see is an erosion of time,
Just look beyond the layers to find,
God's artistry is perfect and complete.
When God peels through the layers he reveals his masterpiece.
Praise God for all the wonders He performs.

Ripley looked at Roseway and smiled. "Wow! It is such a beautiful poem, Rose. Did you write it?"

"Yes, I did. You will understand the poem when you open my present. Open it."

Ripley pulled off the paper. Held within the palm of her hand was a big rock. It was rough and gray with touches of green moss on it, not very nice in appearance. Ripley's face was blank with confusion. Then she asked jokingly, "What, did they have a sale on rocks this Christmas, or is this the rock from my smashed car window?"

Roseway sighed. "No silly, but it is very much a coincidence it would seem. Flip the rock over and you will see what my poem means."

Ripley turned over the ugly rock. Her eyes brightened as the rock sparkled in her hand. "Wow! This is beautiful. It looks like purple diamonds. Is this an amethyst gem?"

Roseway shrugged. "I'm not sure what it is called. See how beautiful it is on the inside of the rock. Yet on the outside it appears so ugly. Look at all the different layers. In the center of the rock is a beautiful gem. I just think that we are much like that rock. When we look at someone, we often judge from what we see on the surface. Take people for example; when we get to know a person and really look into who they are, then we can see so many of their qualities. Often there are many things in a person's life which can make them appear hard and rough on the outside. There must be a hidden gem inside each of us. Sometimes we just have to look deep enough to find it. It just amazes me how God created everything."

Again Ripley shook her head and smiled, amazed. "Well Rose, that is the most unique gift I have ever received. You have a very interesting perspective. I'll treasure it always. Thank you very much. Here, open my gift. It is not very creative, but then I'm not very creative."

Roseway slowly picked away at the wrapping of her present as if to savour the moment. Getting anxious, Ripley tried to hurry her along. Beneath the wrapping was a lovely orange box. It had the word "keepsakes" written on the front. Inside the box was some matching cards for keeping in touch. In the bottom of the box she found a small seashell and an airplane ticket to Florida.

Roseway was a little surprised. "What is this?"

"We are going to vacation on that ocean beach we dreamed about when we were back in Prince George. My mother, Lauren and I are going to Siesta Key in the spring. Mother said you could come too. I told you, Rose, that someday we would get to that beach."

"Oh, I can't believe it. Yes! Yes! Yes!" She said, as she jumped for joy up and down on the bed.

"Thank you, thank you. Woo hoo!"

Ripley was smiling from ear to ear watching Rose's excitement. Rose had such a childlike character that always touched Ripley's heart. It was a priceless moment. Then there was a knock on the bedroom door. Joseph's handsome face peered through the doorway.

"What is all the commotion going on in here?"

Roseway jumped off the bed and ran over to Joseph. "What a surprise to see you. We just finished opening our Christmas presents to each other. I'm going to the ocean with Ripley and her family. It's so exciting. What are you doing here?"

"I know I should have called first, but I wanted to surprise you. There is something important I want to talk to you about. Do you think we could go for a walk?"

Looking at Ripley and then back to Joseph, she asked, "Now? I..."

Ripley interrupted, "Rose, why don't you and Joseph go for a walk. I really should get my mother's car towed into town and get the windshield fixed. I'll do that now. It shouldn't take more than a couple of hours and then I'll be back."

Joseph thanked Ripley for understanding. He grabbed Roseway by the hand and took her downstairs. They put on their coats and went outside. Ripley sat on the bed for a moment feeling a little sombre and disappointed that their great moment was interrupted. For a few moments she sat and looked at the stone sitting in her hand and then reread the poem Rose had written. Then she called a tow truck and went into Kelowna to get the car fixed.

Billy and Sue had caught the bus to Big White for the snowboard competition. Noreen had left to do a shift at the diner where she still worked as the manager.

21
THE SURPRISE

Snuggled together, Joseph and Roseway walked with their arms intertwined, holding hands. It was a bright blue Kelowna sky. The sun made the fresh snow on the trees sparkle like snow ghosts. Roseway was very curious as to what Joseph's important news could be. As they walked, the smile on Joseph's face was pasted in place.

Roseway prodded, "You seem quite pleased with yourself. You haven't stopped smiling since you poked your head around the bedroom door. What is it?"

"What, can't I be happy just to be with you?"

"Of course you can, but I know something is up. I can't stand the suspense any longer. You better tell me soon or else."

"Or else what...Rose?"

"Why I'll..." Roseway stepped away from Joseph, bent down and picked up a handful of snow and shaped it into a firm ball. She threw it at him, hitting him in the head. Joseph laughed at Roseway's playfulness, then picked up a snowball and threw one back. For a few moments, they continued to throw snowballs back and forth until Joseph ran after Roseway and tackled her onto the snowy ground. They lay in the snow laughing. Roseway playfully wanted to make snow angels without marking up the snow. Joseph tried to make the perfect angel but fell over in the snow when he tried to get up. Roseway laughed at Joseph when he came up out of the snow looking like a snowman.

For a moment there was a pause in time as Joseph watched Roseway's expression and listened to her laughter echo through the mountains. Then he pulled her down beside him and looked into her eyes. He slowly moved near to her. Roseway licked the snowflakes from his face. Joseph met her lips and kissed her gently while he spoke softly to her.

"Rose, you are like my own personal snow angel. I am captivated by you. You are special to me, Rose. The first time I saw you, I knew you were different from any other girl I've met. That is what I want to talk to you about."

"Go on, Joseph, and on and on..." she said with dreamy eyes.

"Please Rose, I'm being serious. Let me finish. Since that first day when I watched you asleep in my truck, I knew my heart belonged to you. When you ran away after the fight in the truck, I thought I would never see you again. Since that day, you have constantly been on my mind. Something inside of me wouldn't let you go. With God's help, I found you again. During that time apart, you have grown up. You have been through so much. I see that you are even stronger for it. I am in love with you, Rose, and each day I only learn to love you more. I have something to give to you."

"You have already given me a Christmas present."

"Well, I have something else for you. Just wait here a minute while I get it out of the car...Okay Rose, I don't want you to peek, so I'm going to tie my scarf around your head to cover your eyes. I'll be back in a few minutes."

When Joseph arrived back, he sat in the snow beside Roseway and took her hand and put it inside his coat jacket. Her hand felt the soft fur in his lining. Then he removed the scarf from her eyes and unzipped his coat, pulling out a white cottontail rabbit. He placed it into Roseway's arms.

"What is this, dinner?" She asked with a laugh.

Then she noticed a gold necklace around the rabbit's neck. Dangling from the necklace was a gold ring with a sparkling diamond. Her jaw dropped as she sat speechless and stunned for a few moments. Joseph undid the clasp on the chain and removed the ring. He placed the necklace around her neck and kissed her cheek. Then he lifted Roseway's weatherworn hand and asked her a question.

"Rose, this ring is a symbol of my love for you. I know you have school to finish this year, and there are still many adjustments for you to make. There is no timeline. Since the day I met you, I knew God had brought you into my life. I have come to realize what a precious gift you are to me. Roseway, I would like to spend the rest of my life with you. Do you want to spend your life with me? Will you marry me?"

Holding the rabbit and stroking its soft fur, a tear rolled down Roseway's cheek. She paused for a moment in thought. "Oh Joseph, I want to say yes. With all my heart I want to say yes. I know that I love you, too. I do want to spend my life with you, I do. I just don't feel the time for marriage is now. I need more time to get used to this world. There are so many things I never did as a child. Please understand that I have just found my family again. We are just now beginning to find some of the happiness which was stolen so long ago. I need time to find out who I am as a person, as a woman. It would not be fair to you, for me to give myself to you before I know who I really am. Do you understand what I am trying to say, Joseph?"

"I understand, Rose, that you have felt trapped for a long time. Lord knows I don't want you to ever feel trapped by me or pressured in any way. I'll wait for you, Rose. I'll wait until you know that you are free within yourself to give yourself willingly to me in marriage. I wasn't thinking we would marry right away. I was thinking engagement, and then when you are ready we can get married. If you would prefer, we can just put this ring back on the necklace. You can wear it like this in the meantime. When you are ready to commit to an engagement, then you let me know by putting the ring on your finger. Okay?"

Roseway noticed the disappointment he tried to hide. She smiled at Joseph, trying to ease the awkward tension in the air. "Thank you for understanding. There is one other thing," she said as she put the rabbit in the snow and shooed it away.

Joseph interrupted with a surprised tone, "What are you doing? He is a pet. He is yours to keep. He can't live in the wild."

"Yes Joseph, he can. It is not meant to be caged. It was created to be free. I could not hold it captive."

"But you could shoot and kill it."

"Why would you say that? I'll have you know, I only ever killed for my own survival. To put it in a cage would be much worse than death itself. This kind of creature is meant to be free in the wild. It will adapt to the environment and survive by its God-given instinct."

"Is that right?"

"If it does not survive, at least it will have known freedom."

Joseph hesitated while he thought about what Roseway said. Surrendering his perspective, he said, "Rose, you never cease to surprise me. You really have matured. Okay, if that is what you want to do, we will let the rabbit go free."

They both watched the rabbit run off and hide under a tree. Roseway wrapped her arms around Joseph and kissed him deeply as she thanked him, and then she took off the necklace and handed it back to him. Her eyes sparkled under the winter sky as she

smiled and said, "I'd like it very much if you would put the engagement ring on my finger."

Joseph kicked his feet in the air and put his hands on the top
of his head as a smile lit his face. "So do you want to be engaged?"

"Yes Joseph, I do. Would one year or maybe a two-year engagement be all right with you? I just can't promise a time limit."

"Okay Rose, we can see what the next year brings, whenever
you are ready."

Roseway fantasized out loud. "I think a spring wedding would
be nice, when all the flowers are starting to bloom and the apple
blossoms cover the trees like lace. Everything is made new in the
spring."

Joseph picked her up in his strong arms and spun her around,
kissing her again. Then he put her down and put the ring on her
finger. Joseph grabbed Roseway's hand. As they walked back to the
house, they talked about their dreams; what church they would at-
tend, where they would live, how many children they would have,
and how they would grow old together. They imagined themselves
sitting on a swing on the front porch, playing footsie and sipping
wine as they watched the sun go down behind the mountains.
Excitement grew as they walked and talked. Their feet ploughed
through the snow as they hurried back to the house to tell the news
to someone. Speeding their pace, they began to race toward the
front door.

Playfully Roseway yelled, "First one there gets to tell the
news!" Roseway ran like a gazelle down the driveway, and up the
stairs to open the front door. Joseph was quick on her heels. They
opened the door and Roseway started yelling out names. "Momma,
Ripley, is anyone here?" The house was quiet. "I guess Ripley is not
back yet from getting her car fixed. She shouldn't be that long. I
hope she gets back soon. Momma must still be at the diner where

she works. Billy and Sue won't be back until later tonight. I guess we will have to wait a little longer. In the meantime, would you like something to eat? I could fix up a couple of sandwiches. I'll go put on the kettle and make us some hot chocolate."

Joseph put his hand on his stomach. "That sounds great. I am getting hungry. I'll stoke the fire. It looks like it could use another log. I don't like mayonnaise on my sandwich."

Roseway called back from the kitchen, "This is not a restaurant, you know. Just for the record, don't get too used to me waiting on you. Been there, done that."

Joseph raised his voice so Rose could hear him in the kitchen. "Hey, where is the poker for the fireplace?"

"It should be right there on the stand. Oh, just a minute. I'll find it for you when I bring out the sandwiches. Are men all the same? You can't find anything without a good woman."

Roseway came into the living room with a tray of sandwiches in one hand and two cups of hot chocolate in the other. She barely spoke the words, "The poker stick should be right there." Immediately she dropped the plate and cups onto the floor. There lay Joseph, face down on the floor in front of the fireplace. She ran over to him and went to touch him to look at his face. When she lifted his head, blood stained her hand from a deep cut in the back of his head. Blood mixed with Joseph's shiny black hair.

"No!" She screamed, as she held him in her arms. She then ran over to the phone to call 911. There was no dial tone. A shadow of a man covered the wall in front of her. Roseway slowly put down the phone and turned around. Fear rose within her like mercury in a thermometer. She felt the heat rush through her veins, starting at her toes and working its way upwards, numbing her face. Under her breath she prayed, "Oh God, help Joseph. What do I do?"

The Suprise

ROSEWAY, MY CHILD, THIS IS THE TIME TO CON-
QUER YOUR FEAR ONCE AND FOR ALL TIME. PERFECT
LOVE CASTS OUT ALL FEAR. TRUST IN THE LORD WITH
ALL YOUR HEART AND LEAN NOT ON YOUR OWN UNDER-
STANDING.

Roseway's eyes stared into the dark eyes of Big Joe. He stood
there with the poker in his hand. The shadow on the wall seemed
much larger than the man standing in front of her now. He didn't
seem quite as tall as she had remembered. For a few moments they
just looked at each other, wheels spinning in their minds. Then
Roseway stuttered her first word like a baby speaking for the first
time. "W-what do you think you are doing? You can't go around
hurting people. I'm going to get help for Joseph."

"No, just stop right dare," Big Joe rasped.

Turning to exit the room, Roseway spoke defiantly. "What are
you going to do, hit me with the poker too? Go ahead, hit me."

Big Joe lunged forward, putting his scarred hand on her shoulder. "Wait."

Roseway stopped in her tracks, surprised at his unusual softer
tone of voice. She went to take his hand off of her shoulder. When
she did, she noticed the burn scar on his hand. Suspecting, she
asked, "Are those scars from the cabin fire?"

"Yeah Pumpkin day are. Ya just left me dare to die in dat fire.
Ya must really hate me."

"Well, you are right about that. I do hate you. You are the devil
himself. How could I feel anything but hate toward you? Think
about it. Think about the past twelve years and all you have done.
Out of my way, I'm going to tend to Joseph."

She pulled herself from his grip, leaving him standing there
dumbfounded. He watched her lean over Joseph and very lovingly
care for him. Roseway lifted his head and looked over the wound to

161

assess the damage. Her fingers rubbed the bloody hair from his face, as she whispered "Joseph, wake up—come on, Joseph."

Joseph slowly regained consciousness, wondering where he was and what happened. He looked up at Rose and then over to the little man standing in front of them holding onto a wood poker.

"Why you...you must be Big Joe. If I get my hands on you..." Joseph tried to get up, but his head started spinning.

"Lad, ya best just keep yourself right dare and let me and da lass ave a liddle talk."

Roseway piped up. "There is nothing to talk about, BJ. I want you to leave and never come back. Just leave me and my family alone. I want to get on with my life, preferably without you harassing us all the time. Can't you see that I am a young woman now? I'm engaged to be married. You need to get your own life. I might add, that does not include me in it."

Big Joe stood there thinking about what he wanted to say to her.

22
EYE FOR AN EYE

Ripley had dropped off the car at the auto glass shop. She decided to leave the car there and catch a cab back to the house because they couldn't put the window in the car that day. As the taxi turned onto King Street, she called her mother on her cell phone. The phone rang until the voice message came on saying, "Hello you have reached the home of the Wilks family, please leave your message after the beep."

"Hello Mother, I see you must be out with the bridge club again. I hoped you would be home. I just wanted to tell you that there was a bit of a mishap with your car and I have to get the front windshield fixed. It is in the shop getting a new window put in it as I speak. Also Mother, I wanted to let you know that we will need your credit card to pay for it. I'll be heading back home in a couple of days. Well, I better go now. My cell battery is almost dead. So I'll see you when I get home. Until then, I love you. Bye for now."

When the taxi was about to pull into the Shaffer driveway, Ripley noticed a vehicle parked on the side of the road just down from the driveway. She told the cab driver to drop her off at the end of the driveway. Suspicious, Ripley walked along the hedge by the driveway toward the house. When she neared the house, she decided to peer through the window to spy on Rose and Joseph, to see what they were doing. When she looked in the window, she was astonished to see Big Joe standing in front of Rose holding the poker in his hand. She felt her heart start to pound as she crouched down under the windowsill. Still fresh in her memory was that night in the dark alley when Big Joe knocked her flying to the ground. Her first instinct was to call 911. Hands shaking nervously, she pressed each cold button. Her fingers were clumsy and numb. She could hear the ringing as her call went through. Beep beep. Her cell phone beeped repeatedly. Panicking and scared, she whispered into the phone when an operator said, "Hello."

"Please help. Send a police car over here right away. There is a psycho in the house."

"Is he armed?"

"Yes, he is armed. He is holding a fireplace poker. We may need an ambulance, too. There is a man down. He is lying on the floor holding his head and it looks like he is bleeding."

The phone beeped again.

"Give us your location." The phone beeped again.

"We are in the mountains, just off... Hello, are you there? Hello? Shoot, the battery ran out. Now what do I do?" Ripley sat holding her knees to her chest as her head spun with dismay. What on Earth should I do? I've got to do something before that animal hurts Rose. I'm so scared. God, I need your help. How do I get myself into situations like this? Okay, okay, get a grip. If I could just get in the house and get Noreen's gun, maybe I could at least scare Big Joe away until the police get here. Who knows how long they will take to figure out to come here? I can't wait for them. I could climb up the television antenna and crawl into the window to Noreen's room. Only one thing, I'm afraid of heights. I can do this. I just won't look down.

Ripley proceeded to climb one rung at a time, trying to be as quiet as possible. She kept her focus by keeping her eyes looking up. Reaching the roof, she stepped off the antenna like a cat on the prowl. Her feet stepped quietly along the roof and over toward the balcony outside of Noreen's bedroom. Bravely, she slid down a corner beam to the balcony. Once on the balcony her eyes widened, hoping the sliding door was not locked. With both hands on the door handle she pulled, but it wouldn't open. She bit her lip in frustration. Looking at the window to the side of the door, Ripley made a beeline toward it. *This has to open.* Looking to see if the window was locked, she sighed to realize that it was not.

With all her strength, she tried to push the window open. It didn't budge. *Is it frozen? Why won't it open? Come on God, a little help here would be nice.* Again she pushed, and then pushed again. It moved a little. With determination and all her strength, she heaved the window open wider. She took off her coat and squeezed her slender body through the opening into Noreen's room. The gun was sitting in its place on the rack. Softly she walked over to it. Her face crinkled when the floorboards squeaked. Lifting the gun from the rack, its heaviness surprised her. Ripley was feeling somewhat gun-shy to say the least. Putting her fear aside, she reached for the box of bullets. Her hands were shaking so much that she could hardly put the bullets in the chamber. She put in one bullet after another until the gun was loaded. Her heart was pounding. With her back to the wall, she closed her eyes for a second and breathed in a cleansing breath and breathed out, trying to calm herself.

Okay, I can do this. All I have to do is pretend I know how to use this thing. Big Joe will get scared and run out of the house, and then the police will catch him. Ripley, it is time to put those acting classes from public school to use. I'll just pretend I'm one of Charlie's Angels. It's time to go.

Holding the gun, she charged like a soldier out of the bedroom and toward the railing that overlooked the living room. With the gun pointed at Big Joe, she engaged it with a loud click as to get Big Joe's attention. Joe spun around like a spinning top to face Ripley.

"Well, if it isn't Rose's little friend. I see you recovered from dat liddle bump on your noggin."

"Yes, I did. You caught me off guard that night. That won't happen again. Be assured you are not going to hurt anybody ever again."

Joe went to take a step toward her.

"If you know what is good for you, you won't move again. I swear, I'll pull the trigger and put another hole in your head."

Joe tried to remain calm, but the poker shook in his hand. He could tell how nervous Ripley was, and that made him nervous. He squeezed tight to the poker and leaned on it like it was a cane, to hide his nervousness. Trying to play with Ripley's mind, he taunted her.

"Now dare girl, I don't tink dat would be a good idea to shoot dat gun. What if ya miss? I doubt ya ever fired a gun before. Look at da way you're holding it. All wrong. Dat gun will give ya quite a good kick when ya fire it. I wouldn't be surprised if it knocked your shoulder right out of its socket."

Ripley's voice quivered and her sweating hands shook more. "Shut up, I said."

Roseway spoke up and agreed with Joe for the first time ever. "Ripley, he is right about the gun. Please put it down before someone gets hurt."

Ripley was feeling the anger build along with the fear. Flashbacks of Big Joe hitting her played in her mind like a bad rerun. It did not matter what anyone said at this point in time. She didn't trust Big Joe and was not going to let down her guard for a second.

Ripley defensively raised her voice. "He has a weapon in his hand. Rose, how can you tell me to put down the gun after everything he has done? Look at what he did to Joseph."

Joseph was now holding an ice pack and a towel on his head. Roseway stood. Joseph winced with the pain in his head as he spoke to Ripley. "Rip, please put the gun down and back out of the house and get some help."

"Have you both lost your minds? I'll do no such thing." Looking at Big Joe, she raised her voice with authority. "In fact, Mr. Big Shot, I think there are only two options to choose from. Number one—you put down that poker and you get out of this house and never come back, or Number two—I shoot you right where you stand."

Big Joe took a step toward the staircase, as he answered Ripley's request. "Number one—I'm not leaving until I get to talk to Roseway. Number two—I don't tink ya have da guts to pull dat trigger."

Slowly he kept walking, one step at a time toward the staircase. Each step creaked like an old rocking chair on old floorboards. He took another step. When he reached the third step, Ripley yelled at the top of her lungs. "Stop right there! I mean it!"

Gripped by fear, Ripley felt like her heart was being pulled out of her chest. Her head was spinning with thoughts. *What should I do? I can't let him come any closer. He almost killed me once.* She looked at Big Joe, then looked over at Roseway and then to Joseph sitting on the floor. Then she looked up with a silent prayer of desperation. The gun was shaking in her hands, slippery with sweat. Her finger rested a little tighter on the trigger.

With a crash, the front door swung open, banging against the wall, knocking a picture onto the floor. Pieces of glass scattered. Noreen rushed through the door like a mighty wind. Her eyes met

Big Joe's eyes like darts on fire. Big Joe broke their gaze and within a split second he rushed up the staircase and reached for the gun. Ripley clung to the gun with all her strength. Noreen rushed up the stairs to help get Big Joe from the gun. The three of them tossed around like they were in a wrestling match. The gun sounded like a canon as it fired. Then a thud of dead weight hit the floor, silencing the room. Noreen and Big Joe spun around toward the thud to see...Roseway lying on the floor. They both ran down the stairs to Roseway's side. Noreen rubbed the hair out of Rose's face. "Oh, my baby."

Roseway whispered, "The bullet hit me. I'm bleeding, bad. Am I going to die? Momma I don't want to die, not yet."

"You are going to be fine, honey," Noreen comforted Rose, trying not to show how worried she felt.

Big Joe was putting pressure on the wound with the towel that Joseph had been using on his head. "It looks like da bullet went right through her."

Police entered the front door with their guns drawn. They saw Ripley standing there with the smoking gun and aimed their guns at her. "Put down the rifle!"

Ripley stood stunned for a moment, then pleaded, "Don't shoot me. Don't shoot." With that she threw the gun down to the floor.

Noreen yelled, "Get an ambulance here right away!"

Within minutes, the ambulance arrived. They quickly put an intravenous into Roseway and took her to the hospital. Noreen and Joseph went in the ambulance with her and the paramedics. The police arrested Big Joe after Joseph told them what had happened.

Joseph was treated for his head injury with some stitches and a cold ice pack, and then released. He waited in the recovery room with the rest of the family while Roseway went into surgery. Ripley was taken to the Kelowna Police station where they asked her questions. She called her mother in Prince George and she booked the first flight to Kelowna.

When Annalisa arrived, she talked to the police and they released Ripley into her custody. Ripley walked out of the police station and into her mother's embrace. She cried on her mother's shoulder. "Mother, I'm so glad to see you. Thanks for coming so soon. They interrogated me. I feel like such a criminal. I didn't mean to pull the trigger. It went off so easy. I just touched the trigger and bang. I don't understand what happened. It all happened so fast. How is Rose? Is she going to be all right? I couldn't bear it if she died. I feel so terrible about what happened."

"It happened, dear. You can't take it back. It was a terrible situation. You were doing what you thought was best at the time. From what I heard, you acted quite bravely. I'll take you over to the hospital. Apparently Rose is in surgery now. That is all I know."

Ripley and her mother joined the others in the emergency waiting room where they all sat nervously. The surgeon said that the bullet just grazed Rose's liver and that she had lost a lot of blood. They were waiting to see how her liver was working.

Noreen welcomed Ripley and reassured her that she need not blame herself. "Ripley, I am as much to blame for what happened. It was an accident. We reacted to the situation. We can't change what happened, but we can pray for Rose. Come on honey, please join us."

Noreen gathered the hospital chaplain and a few close friends for a prayer vigil. They prayed through the night. By morning, the head surgeon gave them a good report saying that Roseway would need some time to recover from the wound and loss of blood, but that she would be fine and back to her ole perky self within a few weeks. He said it was a miracle that her liver was not hit. If the bullet had of been a hair closer, she would have bled to death.

Ripley went in to see Rose the next day. Rose was recovering from the surgery. Ripley slipped into the room and poked her head around the privacy curtain, wearing a sheepish grin on her face. "Hello, Rose. Are you feeling up to having a little visitor?"

Roseway lifted her head. A tear ran down her face. "Yes, come over here. You are my hero."

"I don't know what to say to you, Rose. Maybe I should take some gun lessons." She laughed, trying to cover the awkwardness she felt. Her laughter subsided and then there was a moment of silence. Ripley burst forth with explanation. "Things got out of control. The gun went off before I knew what happened. I thought you were in danger."

"I know, Rip. I suppose it looked that way. What is done is done. I don't hold it against you. I know you were protecting me. You are a great friend, Rip. There is just one thing I don't understand. Do you remember the other morning when you blasted me and called me stupid for getting the gun? Whatever possessed you to do that very same thing? At least I know how to use a gun." Roseway laughed, but it hurt. "Rip, if you had of seen your face when you were holding that gun. It was priceless. You were shaking so much. I was afraid the vibration alone was going to trigger the gun."

Ripley was in an aggravated frame of mind. What happened had really shook her up. In retrospect, Ripley agreed. "It must have been funny to watch, but at the time it was quite frightening. I've learned that desperate people do desperate things. I didn't know what else to do. I saw Big Joe and then I saw Joseph on the floor. Big Joe was standing in front of you with a poker in his hand. It looked like you were in danger. I responded without much time to think. Ever since this happened, I have done a lot of thinking about many things. First I was trying to justify my behaviour to myself. In reality, the situation made me totally irrational. Panic can make you react in a way one might not normally react. In my impulsiveness, I almost killed you. I don't know if I would have shot Joe. Thank God I never had to find out. I'd like to think that I would not have shot him. However, if your mom hadn't of come through the door when she did...well, I don't know. I was in a corner. Would that have made me a murderer if I did shoot him dead?"

"No, that would have been self defence."

"Isn't that what society says to defend an action?"

"Ripley, I think you are reading way too much into what happened."

"No, I don't think so. I believe we all have to take responsibility for our actions. Sometimes things are not always as they appear. Take that amethyst rock you gave me. That is a perfect example. At first glance, I thought it was the ugliest rock I'd ever seen. I actually thought you were joking, giving me a rock. When you turned it over and showed me the inside, then I could see the beauty in the rock. I had to look past the exterior and look inside.

"The poem you wrote has a lot of truth in it, too. It does not just apply to me. It can apply to anyone. We are all influenced and changed by our experiences, good or bad. I know that I have been changed in many ways over the last year. Did I want to go through some of the things I went through? No. However, I do realize that these circumstances changed my perspective on things. Even my mother has changed. That is a miracle. There is more understanding between both of us now. My point being, I was thinking about Big Joe. My first impression of him would scare the hell out of Satan himself. However, when Big Joe was tending to your wound, he really responded to you out of care and concern. You were bleeding extensively. He behaved like a concerned father. He actually looked quite concerned about you. It was obvious from the look on his face when the police took him away.

"For that moment as I watched him, I saw him the way Jesus sees him. I think he was like that rock. Nobody, not even me, ever looked beyond that rugged scarred face of his or that raspy voice. Before this happened, I could only see what he did, not who he is. Deep down inside everyone there must be some good. Sometimes I think it is just hidden deep within that person under all those layers of pain, rejection and loss. I have to wonder if the way people treated him when he was young hardened his heart. Is he really any different than anyone else, in that he really just wants to be loved and accepted? The sad thing is the way he goes about trying to find love. It is so wrong. Have you ever asked him about his childhood?"

"No, I told you before; there wasn't much conversation between us. I can't think of him as anything other than what he has always been to me. I don't need to know about his childhood, nor do I want to know. That would be too easy of an excuse for his behaviour. He has to pay for what he has done. Maybe a jail sentence might change him, in the way you say people can be changed. I don't buy it, not for Big Joe. At least not until I see some kind of repentance, justice, some kind of consequence for him. Even a little display of remorse might help change my mind. This conversation is tiring me out. I need to rest now. I'm so tired, Ripley."

"I know you are tired. I'll let you get some sleep. I just hope you know how much I care about you, and that is why I am saying this. I know what it is like to run from pain, from your feelings. Why, I even ran away from my family. It is ironic that I ran away from my family and you were taken from your family. Yet God brought the two of us together to help each other. I pray, Rose, that we will both come to that place of understanding and forgiveness where Big Joe is concerned. I'm not there yet either, but I am curious to know more about Big Joe's childhood."

23
THE TRIAL

The following week, Ripley went home to continue her schooling. Roseway was recovering from her wound and regaining her strength each day. Joseph stayed and visited with Roseway until she was released from the hospital, then he continued driving truck. He stayed at the Shaffer household every chance he had.

For weeks Roseway thought about the conversation she had with Ripley. It was like the prodding of a lamb to go and visit BJ at the jail. Curiosity was getting a grip. She even talked to Noreen about whether or not she should go and visit BJ before the trial started. Noreen tried to persuade otherwise, but left the final decision up to Rose. Roseway questioned her own motives. *Why should I talk to him? All these years, he never talked to me, not really. How can I ever get rid of this bitterness and anger that I have toward him? Would it give me more understanding? Is Ripley right? I think I know in my heart the right thing to do, but part of me just doesn't want to let it go. How can I ever truly be free if I don't face it, face him? God did tell me that I must face my fear. I have the key to open that dungeon gate and allow that little girl to be free. Perhaps by setting Big Joe free by forgiving him, I will be* setting that little girl inside of me free. I think that is what God is telling me. I have to try. With God I can do all things.

Big Joe had already served one month in jail waiting for his trial. He had no bail money to be released. The court of justice was calling for the trial to commence in February. Roseway had her mother drive her to visit him. Noreen and Roseway prayed before she went in. Noreen waited in the hall just outside of the visiting area. Roseway sat in the chair, biting her nails. Big Joe walked in accompanied by a security guard. His appearance surprised her somewhat. She had never seen him so cleaned up. Hair and face were shaved neat. The orange prison suit even brightened up his normally dark eyes. He seemed a lot less intimidating. Big Joe's tone of voice seemed controlled and matter of fact as he spoke.

"Hello Rose. How are you?"

Roseway automatically responded, "I'm fine, feel much better now, just a little tenderness from the wound. I'll have a good scar on my back from the bullet hole."

"Well I never raised ya to be a cry baby, so I reckon ya will get over it soon enough."

"What is wrong with crying? It is a normal response to emotion or pain. God made us that way. Whatever made you think that it is not okay to cry? Were you raised that way?"

"I don't rightly recall. I guess my pa taught me not to be a cry baby. He always said dat cryin was for sissies."

"All these years you never ever mentioned your ma or pa to me. I would like to hear about your childhood, if that is okay with you."

"Why would ya want ta know dat?"

"I'm curious."

"You know what dey say. Curiosity killed da cat. I would like to know one ting doe. Why do ya hate me so much dat ya would leave me ta burn in da cabin fire? Twas a big surprise to awaken with a pounding eadache, only to find myself surrounded by flames. My pant legs were on fire and I tried to put dat fire out wit my ands. Da cabin was too engulfed in flames. So I ran out of dare, rolled around in da dirt till da fire was out. I was in such pain. I crawled down to da stream to cool da burning, and den I cooled me legs wit clay. Don't mind telling ya it took quite some time to heal. Dat was quite da hit on da head ya gave me. I guess ya did learn someting from your Pa after all. Ya know—ya can't go around itting people on da ead." He grinned and almost laughed at his half-hearted joke.

Roseway could only shake her head disgusted at his joke. "I didn't mean for you to catch on fire, but I guess you had it coming. After I hit you on the head, I thought you were dead. After what you did to me, I wished it to be so. Just proves that ya can't keep a bad man down."

"Any ting I ever did was for yur own good. You should know dat. I had ta teach ya some respect. Discipline is a good ting."

"Well BJ, it seems like your method of teaching failed. It would seem that your knowledge in relationships gives very little to speak about. In trying to force people to love you, you make them hate you. When are you going to get it? You can't make people love you. You can't force people to do whatever you tell them to do. When you force yourself on people, it is human nature for them to pull away. It is wrong to just take from others when they say no. Love doesn't just take— it gives, and at the right time it receives."

BJ's face reddened as he tried to respond. "After all dese years, you don't understand me at all."

Rose's tone heightened as she continued to rant on him. "Big Joe, if I don't understand you it is because you never opened up to me. You were too busy criticizing everything I did, while treating me like an animal you thought you owned. What I do know about you is that you are a mean and violent man. You stole me from my family and threatened those I love. You are a criminal and a rapist.

What more do I need to know about you? It disgusts me to think that you are my father."

A crooked smile came across his face as he crossed his arms in defence. "Ah, so your ma told you what happened? Rosy, yur right. I'm all dose tings. However, if I wasn't your pa, ya wouldn't ave bin born. I guess I didn't always treat ya proper. I had to be rough wit ya. It is ard to survive in da wilderness. If you're not tough den ya won't survive. I treated ya dat way cause dat is what I learned from my ma and pa.

Roseway clenched her teeth. "Well Big Joe, that is too bad for you. Telling me this now doesn't really change things. All those years you hardly spoke to me. What difference do you think it makes now?"

"Rosy, I'm hoping ya will come back to da interior wit me some day."

Roseway laughed at his request as if she couldn't believe what he had said. "I'm not coming with you. Neither you nor any army could get me to go with you. You would have to kill me first."

His face darkened. "Ya best be watchin what ya say. You are getting a wee bit cheeky."

Boldness continued to spring forth from the deep. "I'll say whatever I feel like saying. You kept me quiet all these years and now you can hear me out. If you really want a relationship with me, try letting me go. If you care about me, set me free. Show me you love me by being a father who cares enough to love me as an individual person, as someone who also has real needs and desires. My desire is to live here with my mom and then build a life with my fiancé, Joseph. Those days of living in the mountains are finished for me. I can't and won't go back. Turning my life upside down all the time does not draw me close to you." She took a breath and looked him in the eyes and pleaded. "Please try to understand what I am saying."

The room went quiet as BJ broke eye contact and looked away. With a cracking voice he said, "I hear ya."

Roseway was on a roll and she was pouring out her thoughts and feelings faster than he could drink them in—things she had always wanted to say but was too scared. Her tone mellowed. "You know, BJ, we all do terrible things at times. Life's circumstances can either mould us into monsters or saints. It depends on the perspective one takes. You chose to be a monster. I have to tell you this honestly, I don't feel like I could ever forgive you for all the terrible things you have done to me and to those I love. The thing is, I know that God can forgive you. I suppose God knows you better than anyone."

His voice lowered. "Don't ya go talking to me about dat God of yurs. My momma was a bible-believing woman and look what appened ta her and my broders and my pa. Any faith I ad burned down when my ouse fell ta ashes. My God is in da nature. Dis life is all she wrote."

"Well, I dare say that your perspective is a sad one. No hope, no nothing. No wonder you have been such a miserable wretch."

Their conversation was interrupted by the guard telling them their time was up. She would have to come back and visit another time. Big Joe stood like a beaten-down man. His size paled by his shadow. A tear almost wet the corner of his eye as his lip quivered. "Guess you best be on your way den. See ya at da trial."

With a wave, he raised his eyebrow and twisted his lip as he left the room. Roseway went out of the room and collapsed into her mother's arms, and cried with release. She had said many things, but her heart still felt somewhat dissatisfied. A little guilt rested on her shoulder. Freedom was not something she felt yet.

Her curiosity was only more intrigued. What fire? What happened to his family? What happened...?

March arrived and the trial began. It lasted a long three months. The news was abuzz in the small town of Kelowna. Press was all over the story. It was a hot topic and it was personal to the town residents. From salons and churches to the local diner, the story was the subject of conversation. Questions and wagers were made about how much jail time Joe Demerse would have to serve.

The jurors deliberated on the charges against him: one count of rape. Sexual assault is a federal issue in Canada, so federal laws applied. Being that sexual assault is an indictable offence, victims of rape can file and press charges, as long as there is enough evidence to build a case. In Noreen Shaffer's case, there was a police report filed. The Crown Attorney wanted to prosecute Joe Demerse for rape. Other charges included kidnapping and two counts of assault with a deadly weapon.

Joe Demerse took the stand in his own defence. His attorney asked him to tell about his childhood and led him with a few questions. "Where were you born, and can you tell us a little about your childhood?"

"I grew up in Newfoundland. My pa was a fisherman. He was always out on da sea, sometimes for weeks on end. While he was away at sea, Momma did her best to take care of us boys, me and my two broders. Money was tight. We mostly lived on stew and fish. Sometimes the catch was a poor one and pa would come ome with only a couple a bucks in his pocket. Tension in da ouse ran igh most of da time. Pa would spend da money on cigarettes and booze. Momma would argue. Pa would put her in her place doe. I remember dat night dat Pa beat my momma up bad. He hit me and my broders too and sent us to our beds. Momma cried herself to sleep. I could hear her sobbing true da din walls. It appened all da time.

"Dat night I sneaked out of my bedroom. I was about six years ole den. I made up my mine ta run away. So I packed a grocery bag wit clothes and went to my secret fort dat me and my broders made. I slept dare dat night. In da morning I eard sirens and wondered what all da commotion was about. When I realized da commotion was at my ouse, I ran as fast as I could back to my ouse. It had burned to da ground wit my family inside. Papa passed out from da booze and his lit cigarette fell onto da sofa and smouldered. Smoke moved true da house killing my broders, Ma and Pa. I never taught about it much, until being in dat cabin fire myself."

There was nervousness in Big Joe's voice as he looked over to Roseway and continued the story. "Down by da river, down from dat ole cabin, my ands and legs burned in agony. I had a lot of time to tink. Memories from when I was a boy flashed in my mind. Like I said, I was just a little boy not much more den six years ole, the age Rose was when I took er from er momma."

Still looking over to Roseway he said, "Rose, dare are many tings ya don't know bout me. Ya lived wit me all dose years, but ya never got to know me. All dose memories I kept buried all deese years. It made me wonder, why ya had come ta hate me so much dat ya would hit me over da head and leave me for dead? It kind of showed me how I ad treated ya."

The Crown Attorney objected, saying it was irrelevant, and moved to have Joe's last statement stricken from the record. The judge sustained the motion.

Roseway sat in the courtroom astonished at the story Big Joe told. For the first time she felt a little pity toward him. Her own conviction of violent intent was very real.

Defence continued to question Joe. "What happened to you after your family died in the fire?"

"I stayed wit my grandma for a while, but I guess she couldn't andle me no more in her ole age. So she ad me put in da foster ome. Ya could say I bounced from one ome to da next. Didn't seem anyone wanted me. One of da foster parents hit me with a hot iron when she got so mad at me. The iron hit my face and dat is ow I got dis scar. Den when I was fifteen I took off and hitch-hiked from one town to da next, working odd jobs. Most people shunned me cause of da scar on my face. Day wouldn't hire me for work cause day tought I was too dumb. Never finished igh school, ya know? So I bounced from one town to da next trying to find whatever work I could get. When I reached Kelowna I did get a few jobs. I kind of took a likin to Noreen. I taught she liked me too, da way she always flirted wit me. I got too carried away wit her dat night. When she hit me wit da hot coffee, I guess I kinda snapped. I suppose dat is when I raped her. I don't really remember what I did after getting hit wit da coffee. It was in da local newspapers soon enough. Da police was lookin for me. I put two and two together and then I went inta hiding for a while."

"Would you say that you black out from time to time?"

"Ya I guess dat is about da jist of it. It seems dat on a few occasions I blacked out over da years, usually when someding shocking appened or someding made me really angry."

"Did you know Rose was your daughter when you abducted her?

Joe sighed. "Well ya, I assumed she was. I'm smart enough dat I can count to nine. Dat is why I took her. It might ave been a liddle selfish of me, but I wanted a family. Losing my family so young, left me feelin very alone. I was tired of being alone all da time and hiding from everyone. I didn't tink Noreen would miss da kid since she ad two others. Actually, I was doing her a favour taking Rose— one less mouth for her to feed. I didn't really tink it through. I just got da idea in my head and acted on it. Didn't quite know what I was getting myself into. Once I had taken Rose wit me, dare was no turning back. I raised her da way my parents raised me. I don't tink it hurt her any. She is a pretty good kid."

The prosecution objected and the judge overruled. Later, defence cross-examined Roseway and made it appear like Big Joe saved her life and that he actually raised her to be quite knowledgeable and independent, having many survival skills.

Ripley's testimony was very much in favour of the Crown. Evidence showed that Joe Demerse had a history of violent behaviour. Defence repeatedly tried to shoot down any un-witnessed accusations by saying it was hearsay.

The defence gave a convincing summation, claiming their client pleaded guilty to the charges as he remembered the occurrences. Defence appealed to the court to take under consideration Joe's emotional state of mind as unbalanced because of the traumas in his childhood, stating that with professional counselling Joe could be helped.

The Crown called Rose, Noreen, Ripley and Joseph as their key witnesses. The Crown presented a very strong case against Joe. They highlighted every wrong he had done, showing him to be the worst of criminals. They utilized the rape, the abduction, and Joe's verbal and physical abuse to Roseway while she was in his care. They stated that Joe Demerse was a danger to society. No amount of jail time could cure him of his anger and his blackouts. Ripley's detailed description of Joe's attack on her reinforced to the jury Joe's violent nature and unstable mindset.

The defence had played their trump card in claiming that Joe was emotionally unstable due to his childhood and that he suffered from blackouts beyond his control. Through the testimony of Dr. Richard Birmingham, they concluded that with extended counselling, Joe would be no threat to society.

When the Crown finished their summation, they pleaded that Joe be sent to prison. "An eye for an eye. Pleading for a conviction and at least a twenty-year jail sentence, for the years he's stolen from Rose and her family."

The jurors listened to testimony after testimony. When the jury was in deliberation, one of the male jurors, Tom James, empathized with Joe after hearing his story. He argued that the kidnapping charge should be dropped because Joe was Rose's father. Juror Judy Boyle sympathized more with Noreen Shaffer's testimony and the rape, but that did little to influence the other jurors.

After four days of deliberation, the jury rendered the verdict. Judge Stanton read the verdict. "On the charge of kidnapping, the verdict is guilty. For the charge of raping Noreen Shaffer, the verdict is guilty. Two counts of assault with a weapon—guilty. The court has found Joe Demerse guilty on four counts out of four and therefore he is sentenced to serve twenty years in prison at the Fraser Regional Correction Centre in Maple Ridge, British Columbia. During this time of imprisonment, the court finds it necessary for Mr. Demerse to undergo continued psychological counselling. A psychological review will be done in four years. The review of his psychological state of mind will have to show evidence of significant change if there is to be any chance of early parole. The court is adjourned."

The courtroom was ecstatic with noise, mostly cheers of victory and congratulations. Roseway suddenly didn't know what she was feeling. She smiled with the rest of them. Joe looked at Roseway from across the room. He never broke his gaze as he stood there in handcuffs and then was lead out of the room. Roseway felt a lump in the pit of her stomach. After all the years of feeling hatred for him, now she felt an emotion that was very unfamiliar to her. In a way it was like a cord that had held her up for so many years had been broken. Yes, she felt like a stronger person. The fear that had kept her captive all those years, she had conquered. That little girl was let out of that dungeon, and Roseway knew that she had walked through it. The realization was so clear. She pondered, Why do I feel sad? Is it guilt or conviction? Deep down, it bothered her that Big Joe was going to his own dungeon. Perhaps one has to go to that place of confinement to someday walk out changed by the experience—to be made even stronger in weakness and vulnerability. It is kind of ironic that my freedom has taken him to prison. What is freedom, anyway? Isn't freedom really just a frame of mind? I can be free to do whatever I wish. At the same time, I could be chained emotionally to my past. In that case I would not be totally free. God, you said I had the power to break the chains. It must be a matter of the will. It is up to me to choose to be free. The only way I can be free is to accept the past, and forgive the wrongs Joe has done. Lord, it is so very difficult to let go completely.

Ripley nudged Roseway out of her deep thought. "Well Rose, I guess we don't have to worry about Big Joe bothering you anymore. Isn't that great?"

With an unsure expression, she convinced Ripley that she agreed. "Yeah...Yeah...I suppose you are right. Let's get out of this place."

24
SIESTA KEY

The trial had finished and both Ripley and Roseway had gone back to school. Ripley finished her first year of college, and Roseway completed her classes with the tutor. Rose's mathematics and English skills had improved at an incredible pace.

Ms. Wilks planned a wonderful vacation for the three girls at a resort on the sandy beaches of Siesta Key. They arrived just in time for the Siesta Fiesta, a weeklong celebration. For Roseway, it was like she had stepped off the plane onto another planet. Watching out of the car window, she commented on the funny-looking trees. Ripley told her they were palm trees. She teased Roseway for her naivety. "Rose, you better watch out that the monkeys don't throw coconuts at you from the trees."

Roseway replied, hanging on every word Ripley said to her, "Really, there are monkeys? It is so different from back home. I can't wait to get to the beach. First thing we are going to do is run down to the water and dip our feet in the ocean."

"You have to be careful you don't step on a jellyfish."

"Why?"

"Because they can hurt and they are poisonous. But don't worry; just keep an eye out for something that looks like jelly."

Just before they reached the ocean resort, Ripley fell asleep in the car. She had her head leaning back in her seat and her mouth open in a relaxed state. Thinking it to be funny, Roseway slipped a grape in Ripley's open mouth. It startled her awake. She almost choked on the grape.

"What the...? Who did that?"

Roseway couldn't hide her guilty expression as she started to laugh at Ripley's response.

"It's not funny."

Ms. Wilks and Lauren laughed too. Ripley insisted it was still not funny. "You wait, Rose; paybacks are a...well, you just wait."

They checked into the Sands Beach Resort and took their bags up to the room. Excited, the two girls dropped their bags and bolted out the door. "Mother, we are going to check out the beach. See ya in a bit."

Running across the beach and through the thick sand, they kicked off their shoes, lifting up sand all the way. Roseway was mesmerized by it all. She commented on everything. "Look at the white sand. It is as white as snow. It reminds me of the snow back home. Look at the ocean. Do you smell the salty air? Seashells lay on the shore like leaves."

Both of them went into the water. It rushed up over their feet. Together they splashed in the waves with smiles and laughter echoing down the beach. Ripley just watched Rose. She loved her innocence, the way she made everything seem so amazing and new. It felt spiritual in essence. Ripley was intrigued by the way Rose made her want to experience life with a fresh outlook. Ripley always seemed a little sceptical about anything that seemed too good to be true. Losing all sense of time, the two of them sat in the sand talking as the late afternoon shadows cooled their arms.

Roseway lead into the conversation. "How is Professor Cleveland?"

"Oh, you mean John D."

"Well well, so we are on a first name basis now?

"Yes, we are. I finished my first year and John won't be my teacher next year. I have to tell you that I have been on a few dates with him. I really like him. There is definitely chemistry between us. However, when it is time for him to drop me off and kiss me goodnight, I feel a little uncomfortable—afraid of getting too close, I think. You know, I have not been with a man since I was raped. I find it frustrating not being able to respond to him in a more passionate manner. I think he feels the hesitation coming from me. There is another thing that happened in my past which I have kept secret. In some ways that experience has brought some confusion. I'm just trying to process all of it along with my feelings. Maybe someday I'll tell you more. I have not come to that place yet, where I feel free to share it all. I guess there is still a little bit of shame hidden within me."

Roseway paused as she thought about what Ripley said. "Well, if you are thinking that what you have done is so bad you can't talk about it with your best friend, then maybe you should talk to a counsellor. Definitely you need to be open with your boyfriend. He should know how you are feeling. Have you told him anything?"

"He knows that I was raped, but I have not told him everything, or how it's making me feel. I don't know how he will react."

"I'm sure he will understand. Maybe he can help you overcome these feelings you are having."

"You could be right," Ripley said while rubbing her head.

"Is there something wrong?"

"Oh, I still get these headaches sometimes. I thought they would go away, but they seem to be getting more frequent."

"Have you been to the doctor and asked him about it?"

"Not with the trial and then school. I just haven't had the time to go back for a check-up."

"I don't want to sound like your mother, but it might be a good idea."

"Yeah, yeah, I'll make an appointment when we get back. Are you and Joseph still thinking of getting married next spring?"

"I'm not really sure. I think it is still a little soon. I love him, but I'm not ready to leave Momma. There are still many things we have to do—things that we missed out on."

"If Joseph loves you, then he will wait until you are ready. If you are unsure about getting married, I think you should wait."

Lauren interrupted their deep conversation. "Are you girls going to sit on the beach like two bumps on a log all day, or are you coming with Mother and me? We are going out for dinner. Come on. Get your butts in gear."

Behaving like two young schoolgirls, they both giggled and joked as they followed Lauren back across the beach to the hotel.

Bright and early the next morning, they were up and out for a full day; breakfast at the Bay Club and then a tour of the Bay on the Siesta Cruise. Dinner and dancing followed. They had a wonderful time spending a couple of days by the pool and relaxing on the beach, making sand castles.

Ms. Wilks loved to read a steamy novel and Lauren loved to shop. They spent a day at St. Armand's trying on clothes in the many different shops. Then they tried fine dining at the Prego Bistro, and then went back to the hotel for some night-time fun at the local dance spot. This made a satisfying end to the day.

They exhausted themselves enduring a full schedule of fun-filled days, and were soon ready to return home. Packing up their suitcases with souvenirs, new clothing and a few gifts, they prepared for their early flight the next morning. It was ten o'clock and they were ready to turn in for the night when the phone rang. Ms. Wilks answered and listened for a moment. Then she asked a few questions. "What? When did this happen? How did this happen? You've got to be kidding. That is terrible. Yes, yes she is right here."

Ms. Wilk's face turned pale with worry as she looked over to Roseway. "My dear, your mother is on the phone and she wants to talk to you. I'm afraid she has some rather alarming news to tell you."

Roseway took the phone into her hands and placed it up to her ear with a disturbed look on her face. Noreen began to talk to Rose. "Hello honey, how was your trip?"

"Mom, it has been wonderful. We have done so many fun things, but somehow I don't think that is why you are calling. What is the matter?"

"You are right, Rose. I don't know how to tell you this."

"Just say it. What is it?"

"Oh baby, it is about Joe Demerse. I'm sorry to tell you that this afternoon the guards at the prison found him in his cell unconscious. They tried to bring him back, but it was no use. He had been unconscious too long and did not get enough oxygen to his brain. He passed away today."

"Why was he unconscious? Did another inmate try to kill him?"

"No, it wasn't that. Apparently Joe tried to hang himself with a bed sheet. He is gone, honey. There will be an autopsy done to confirm the cause of death." There was a silent pause on the phone. Noreen interrupted the quiet. "Are you okay?"

"I'm shocked. Why would he do that? He always seemed like such a tough guy. It doesn't make any sense to me. It is not like him at all."

"We don't always know why people do the things they do. He must have been in a dark place. Maybe he thought taking his life was the only way out?"

"That is such a cop-out, Mom. He made one selfish choice after another. So why should I be surprised that he would end his life only thinking of himself?"

"How can you judge him, Rose? You were not in his shoes, nor do you have any idea what he felt or what he was feeling. It is not right to assume you know what he was going through emotionally."

"Why are you defending what he did?"

"Rose, I'm not defending him or his choices. I'm just saying that no one will ever know what compels a person to take their own life. I suppose you have the right to feel angry with him. Anyway, he has no other family. What do you want to do?"

"As crazy as it is, I guess because I am his only living relative that we should arrange some kind of funeral for him."

"There is one other thing. Joe left a note. I have not been to the prison to find out what is in the note. When you get back, you and I will go to the prison and get the note and the rest of his belongings. I have to make a few calls to see what else I can find out. I'll go for now and talk to you tomorrow. Try to get a good night sleep. I love you."

"Okay Mom, I'll see you tomorrow. I love you, too. Bye."

Ripley got up off the couch and went over to Roseway to give her a hug. "Mother told me what happened. What a surprise. How are you feeling?"

"I don't really know. I'm feeling kind of numb right now. Somehow it just doesn't seem real. I think I would like to be alone right now. If you don't mind, I'm going to go to bed."

"Are you sure you don't want to talk about it?"

"Thanks, but not right now. I think I just need some time to process this."

Feeling many opposing emotions, Roseway went off to her bedroom. Lying in the quiet of her bed, she looked up at the ceiling, biting her hand to keep from crying. Still, a small tear slid from her eye down her cheek into her ear. Neither words nor thoughts could pierce through the wall she was building around her heart. She could not speak to God, for want and need were frozen deep within her spirit. Silence was her companion and that is how she wanted it to be. In a way, it felt comforting to visit that valley of despair again. It was as familiar to her as the drug of pity. Her childhood companion of dark emotion had returned to her. She wrestled with it all night long, tossing like the waves on a stormy ocean.

* * *

They caught the early flight back to Prince George, where Roseway would get a connecting flight back to Kelowna. The conversation was at a minimum, and that was bothering Ripley.

"Rose, are you going to talk to me? We have been flying for two hours and you have hardly said a word."

"What do you want me to say? Do you want me to break down and cry or shout hip-hip hurray? Honestly, I'm not trying to purposely shut you out. I can't talk about it or I might just fall apart. I didn't sleep last night for thinking. So many things were running through my mind."

"What kind of things? Tell me how you are feeling? What can I do to help?"

"There is nothing you can do—nothing anyone can do. I have to sort things out in my head. That is what I have been trying to do. I can't paint some lovely picture of the time I spent with Big Joe. For so long I just wanted to escape from him. Now that he is gone forever, I can't help but think that maybe I was so blinded by tunnel vision that I never recognized anything good about him. In my thinking I realized a few things. The trial brought up some valid points. I suppose he did teach me some good things. Are they valuable lessons? Genetically, I will have some of his traits. If I think him to be a bad man and even if I still loathe him, does that make me a bad person? Does it make me any different from him?"

"Rose, I think you are a great person. You have always had strength about you that most people strive to have. You have a God-given gift. Maybe Big Joe was the vessel used to help develop those strengths. Yes, he was your father whether you liked him or not. Whatever you feel at this time is okay. You will work it out."

Roseway crinkled her forehead. "In a way, my perspective of Big Joe has been blown apart. All these years I saw him as mean and hard, even a frightening monster. After hearing his story, I know he was always just a socially isolated coward on the run. Now that he has taken his own life, I see him as a scared, lonely, sad person who was not strong enough emotionally to handle his despair. He really was alone in that jail. God was not someone he leaned on to help him. I have such mixed feelings. One minute I pity him. The next minute I might even be relieved that I don't have to worry about him turning my life upside-down anymore. At other times I even miss him. On top of it all, I even feel guilt. It's crazy."

"Rose, I think it is normal to have conflicting thoughts and emotions. You have been on an emotional roller coaster for a long time. Be patient, pray, and allow yourself to grieve in whatever way you need to grieve. As for Joe, we don't know what he was thinking in that jail."

"I know what you are saying. However, the guilt I am feeling weighs heavy. I can't help but feel that I shouldn't have been so mean to him. I am the Christian. The last time I spoke to him I wasn't very nice. I said many hurtful things. Do you think that the things I said pushed him to make that decision to kill himself?"

"If that is what is weighing you down, don't let it. You can't take back what you said to him. Trying to put a guilt trip on yourself is not going to bring him back. It is not going to do you or anyone else any good. So just stop it. For whatever reason, Big Joe made that decision, no one else. We can't live on what-ifs. Don't let the devil twist things around.

"Rose, you have come such a long way from when I first met you. Maybe you said things to him that you shouldn't have said or maybe you had a right to say them. Give those things to God and leave them there. It is okay to grieve his death. It is okay to realize that possibly there is a part of you that loved him. In his own twisted way, maybe he did love you. Maybe he didn't know how to show it. Look at the example of his father, perhaps not the best teacher. I'm not trying to paint him a saint by any stretch of the imagination. Sometimes, if we try to look at people through the eyes of Christ, then we may see a totally different perspective. You taught me that, Rose. So don't allow yourself to go back to that place of bondage again. Don't allow him to have power over you from his grave. Forgive him and yourself and be free of it all. Will you think about it?"

"Ouch, Ripley. You haven't lost your knack for being direct and to the point. I wish it was so simple to just forgive and forget, but it is not. It is human nature to hang on to our hurts."

"I wasn't saying to forget everything. We have the power and strength to overcome all things through Christ Jesus. We don't deny the truth, but we do allow the truth to set us free. Make a choice to allow God to carry you through the storm. That is enough preaching for one day. Rose, you know I care, and that is why I'm real with you."

"Rip, you never cease to surprise me. You have really learned a lot going to church. Thanks for the advice." Roseway gave Ripley a little punch on the shoulder.

The seatbelt sign came on and the captain of the plane said to prepare for landing. They walked off the plane and all said their goodbyes. Roseway thanked Ms. Wilks and told Ripley she would give her a call when she returned home.

24
REDEMPTION

Noreen met Roseway at the airport and they talked during the drive home. Noreen told Roseway that she went and picked up Joe's belongings and managed to get a copy of the note that he left for Rose.

"Why did you go without me, Mom? I thought we were going to go together."

"Well, honey, I just thought that it would prevent any unnecessary hurt. Why torture yourself by going to the prison? I went and did what needed to be done. It took about a half an hour and I was out of there and on the way back home."

"What does the note say?"

"Honestly, I never read it. I thought you should be the one to read it. After all, he left it for you. There is a beautiful lookout up ahead. Why don't we stop there?"

There was a light breeze in the air. They stepped out of the car and walked over to a picnic table where they sat down. Roseway took a deep breath as her eyes roamed the landscape. Blue-bodied water from the lake in the distance almost looked like it was painted in. From a distance, the green pine trees looked like moss around the shore's edge. She closed her eyes for a moment, feeling the sun on her face. Her thoughts were still a little clouded. She was feeling apprehensive about reading the letter, fearing the unknown. She breathed a few cleansing breaths and silently spoke. God, please give me the strength to read this. Give me an open mind to receive from it whatever it is I need to hear from Big Joe and from you.

Noreen passed Roseway the brown paper bag. There was not much in it, just an old chequered shirt and a pair of worn-out jeans, his boots and a couple pages of paper. Roseway looked at the shirt and rubbed her hands on it. She lifted it to her nose and smelled the material. It had a familiarity about it. It somehow made her feel connected to him. She left the shirt lying on her lap and she reached for the papers. Noreen gently grabbed her arm. "Are you sure you want to read it? No one will blame you if you don't."

Roseway replied in a soft whisper. "Yes, Mom, it is the least I can do. I want to know what he was feeling, what he thought. I just feel that there is a bigger reason than I can fathom. Maybe the answer is in this letter."

Roseway opened the crinkled letter. An old picture fell out onto the ground. Picking it up, Roseway stared in disbelief. "Momma, this picture survived the cabin fire. He must have found it and kept it with him all this time. It is a picture he took of me and him when we went fishing. He set up his camera and put it on automatic. I remember him running to get in the picture. We held up this fish I caught. He liked to take pictures and develop them in the cabin. BJ always said it was magic making the picture come to life.

"I never thought him to be the sentimental type. I never told you, but he had pictures of all of us. He hung them on the walls in the cabin. Those pictures were all I had of you, Billy and Susie. I thought they all burned except for the one that I found. He must have found this one and kept it." She passed the picture to Noreen and paused another moment, and then began to read aloud.

Redemption

Dear Rose,

Well, if you are reading my letter, den I guess I'm dead. I didn't do it to make ya sad. I tought I best say a liddle someting to ya. In dis prison dare is a lot of time to spend tinking about tings. If ya knows me a tall, den ya would know how much I hate being caged like an animal. I like da mountains, da trees and just being outdoors. Being locked in dis room is not livin. I probably deserve it dough after what I did. Someting ya said a while back kinda stuck in my mind, "dat ya always tried to escape me." At da time I never understood. I tink I know now. I hate to tink ya felt like I felt in dis prison, dat I did dat to ya. I want ya ta know dat I was always proud of ya even doe I never showed it.

Roseway lifted her head for a moment, choking back her tears, trying to hold in any emotion. "Those words would have meant so much to me, had I heard them from him before. Now, why would he tell me this now?"

Noreen sighed, trying to find an acceptable reason. "God works in mysterious ways. When Joe was alone and in prison, I'm sure he thought about his life and realized many things he would have done differently."

Roseway rubbed her eyes and looked down at the paper and continued to read. *Dar is a chaplain who visits da inmates and he came a knockin on me door one day. I didn't want ta talk ta him, but he seemed a nice enough fella. Besides at dat point any company was welcome. Better den starin at da four walls. He did da God talk. Twas as if ya told him what ta say. He talked about Jesus in da same way you do. He said dat God loved me and could forgive me sins. He left me a liddle booklet about acceptin Christ as me Saviour. I told him dat I'd ave a look at it. Den he left and I suppose he went to visit da other inmates.*

I can't take back da tings I done. I don't regret da years I had wit ya. Dose were good days for me; to see me daughter grow into a fine and feisty young woman. Now I also know what it must ave been like for your momma, not havin ya in her life. Cause I missed ya not being in my life, da last couple of years. Ya once tried ta talk ta me about redemption. I didn't tink much about it den. But like I said, being in dis place, dat is all one has to do is tink. I've never bin much of a prayin man, as ya well know. If I could pray a prayer it would be dat ya wouldn't hate me anymore. If dar is a God, my hope is dat ya both would forgive me for da bad tings I done.

I want more den anyting to live back in da mountains. It wouldn't be da same witout you doe. I can't see me spendin da next fifteen to twenty years in dis place. I'd be crazy by den. All da tinkin I've been doing, I realize many tings. So my Rose, I want ya ta be free. Ya said if ya love someting, let it go free. It would be best if I was not around. Dat way, I can't turn your life upside down anymore. So I'm hoping dat if ya are reading dis letter dat I am on my way ta da blue bayou or maybe ya call it eaven. I'm oping dat God will forgive all me sins and even me taking me own life. If dis is da case den ya can lay me ashes up in da river up by da ole cabin. Den I'll be at rest. In doing so, I'll know dat ya spent one more day up in da mountains wit me. Den ya can say a proper good-bye. Good-bye Rose. Don't ya be a cryin no more Rose. Cryin is for sissies.

Luv, Your Dad—Big Joe

"Oh Momma, it is my entire fault. How can I ever live with myself? I was so mean to him the last time I talked to him. I gave him no hope for a future. I'm saddened by it all."

"Rose, don't do this to yourself. In his own way, he tried to show you that he loved you. He wanted you to be free. It was his choice. You didn't tell him to commit suicide. Look at what he wrote in the back of this booklet."

Hoping desperately, Roseway responded, "Do you think he has been redeemed? Do you think he is in heaven?"

"Well, I don't really know dear. That is not for us to judge. Only God knows the answer to that question."

"Momma, I think I can forgive him now. Can you?"

Noreen paused, surprised by the question. "Honestly, I don't know. I never really thought about forgiving him. Like you, I spent so many years despising the man. Part of me does feel pity for him now. God says to forgive those who hurt us and God will forgive us."

"Are you saying that it is as simple as making a choice to forgive?"

"Yes, I believe that is what God is telling us. It may not be an easy thing to do, but it is a simple concept to follow. When we forgive, we are allowing God to heal us. In the process we are setting ourselves free from the hurt. I believe forgiveness can help us move forward in life."

"Momma, what do you say we head home now? I have a few phone calls and arrangements to make."

25
GOODBYE...DAD

A small handful of people gathered at the memorial service. Roseway put on a pretty flowered dress and wore her long hair in a braid up off of her face. She looked like an angel as she sat in the chair in front of the casket. Her face radiated confidence and strength. Noreen was dressed in her favourite shade of blue. Joseph looked more handsome than ever with his black hair combed back, dressed in a fitted black knit sweater and dress pants. He held Rose's hand throughout the service. Ripley also made it down for the funeral, not as much for Big Joe, as for Rose. Something still made her feel uncomfortable about all the things and people he had hurt. Perhaps it was the lingering headache that seemed to hang on like a burr to wool.

The pastor of Noreen's church, Pastor Reid, read a few scriptures. He led them into a few prayers and said a small sermon. "Today, we gather before the Lord God, the Creator of all things. We say our goodbyes to Joe Demerse. Some knew him well. He was the son of John Demerse and Evelyn Demerse; the brother of Todd and Jacob. All are also deceased. They knew Joe when he was a young boy.

"Joe was the father of Rose Shaffer. Some may think of this service as nothing more than a ritual, to show a little respect for the dead. Some wouldn't call it respect. Whatever this service is about is between you and the deceased and God. Perhaps to some this service may be an opportunity to put some closure to the end of a relationship between yourself and Joe? If one were to look at the life of Joe Demerse, one might see only the negative in his life. God not only sees the bad things in a person's life, he also knows and sees the good. God is full of grace, love, mercy and forgiveness. This one man's life has changed the lives of many people here today. I challenge you to look for the good things that have happened in your life because of the life of Joe Demerse.

"Many times in life we wonder why we have to endure hardships. It is said that God has a purpose for all things. If we look closely enough, we may see that God will reveal the blessings that are easily overlooked or taken for granted. I have talked to the family and know of your friendships, which in essence and in all probability would not be in existence today, if Joe Demerse had not existed. Lives became intertwined because of the choices he made so many years ago. In the midst of the storms, God works his miracles. He brings healing and restoration to broken relationships. The old things become new. In the lesson of what appeared to be an ugly rock, we always have a choice to look beyond the surface and see the precious gem. The perspective we take about life or death will decide the choices we make. When someone dies, it always makes us look at life from a new perspective. May the life and the death of Joe Demerse open us up to a new perspective of the meaning of life and how we live our lives. May the choices we make be ones that affect other people in our lives in a positive way. Ashes to ashes and dust to dust, God formed man from the dust of the earth and to the earth man shall return. To God, we commit Joe Demerse's spirit, now and forevermore. Amen.

EPILOGUE

Roseway finished reminiscing about their lives and what brought them to that place where together they sat on that rock watching the flowing river. After a few moments of quiet repose, Roseway stood and emptied the small container of ashes into the wind, where it blew across the water. Little minnows swam to the surface. A silver fish jumped high out of the water, then disappeared into the flow. Roseway sat staring at the ripple in the water that seemed to go on and on. Without even realizing it, she whispered, "Goodbye...Dad."

Joseph nudged her in the arm to snap her out of her daze. "What is it?" he asked.

A smile graced her face as she replied, "Oh, it was an old friend of mine." Joseph put his arm around Rose. Ripley put her arm around Rose's other shoulder, and the three of them turned to walk away.

Looking at her two special friends as if she discovered a great revelation, "You know what, Joseph, Ripley? I can't believe all that we have been through and how our lives have changed in the last few years. I remember sitting in that meadow and praying like it was only yesterday. I was a child with broken innocence, afraid and desperate. When I prayed that prayer, God found me with only an offering of my tears. Only now can I look back and see how God has answered my humble cry. I recognize His hand working in all of our lives. Now we see the bigger picture put together piece by piece. We see the changes which came through our experiences. There is an unspoken assurance that whatever the future has in store for each of us, we don't have to walk the road alone. That road will never end as long as we have Jesus as our Lord and Saviour."

There was a quiet hush as they stood silent on the rock watching the ashes disappear.

Roseway broke the silence once again. "On another note, you know what else I'm thinking?"

At the same time both Ripley and Joseph replied, "No, what?"

"Now that I inherited this land, someday I'd like to come back and rebuild that cabin. Wouldn't that be a nice summer thing to do? It was the only thing Big Joe owned. Joseph, maybe we could get married up here. Have about six kids, live off the land."

Ripley said, "Rose, you are a dreamer. What will we ever do about you?"

Roseway asked, "Isn't that what life is all about, making dreams come true?"

Joseph said truthfully, "We can only dream the dreams. God makes them come true."

The sequel *Ripley* is the next book in The Narrow Road series.

Decision

You can begin your new life in Jesus Christ today.

My Decision to receive Christ Jesus as My Saviour

Name:

Date:

I confess to you, God, that I am a sinner, and ask you, Jesus, to forgive my sins. I ask you to take total control of my life by becoming my Lord and personal Saviour. I ask you to walk with me always and lead me through all the days of my life. I believe that you are the Christ and that you died for my sins on the cross and that you were raised from the dead for my justification. I do now receive you and confess you, Jesus, as Saviour. Thank you for walking the road of sacrifice for me.

About the Author

With twenty years' writing experience, creative writing classes, and workshops, Rebecca compiled an anthology of her poetry called *Inspirational Poems of the Heart*. She has also recorded a CD of music titled Greater Love.

Rebecca's first book was published in 2005. *When Times Stands Still* is said to be like a moment in time for each of us to experience. It is a fresh, personal autobiography with a short chapter format with a bible study for each chapter. It was written under the pen name Rebecca Hickson and can be purchased on Amazon or through Xulon Press.

In five years, Rebecca's pen has been flowing. The anticipated arrival of *The Narrow Road* series is hot off the press. *Roseway: The Road that Never Ends* is the first book in the series. The sequel, *Ripley: The Road of Acceptance*, and the third book in the series, *Jenn: The Road of Sacrifice*, are riveting fiction novels covering a wide variety of modern-day topics.

Soon to be available is the biography of Jeneece Edroff, who was nominated to the Oprah Winfrey Show as one of the most amazing kids. She was also inducted into the Terry Fox Hall of Fame, and is the youngest recipient to have been awarded the Order of British Columbia. Her biggest struggle in life is against a threatening disease known as Neurofibromatosis. Years of major back surgeries, pain, medications and tumours have not kept this young visionary from reaching many milestones. She has motivated a country by her enthusiasm, and has raised millions of dollars for a variety of charities. Her true-life story is an example of paying it forward.

Author's Artist Statement

In my writings I try to convey the message about the ultimate amazing love and hope we can have through Christ Jesus. My prayer is that all who read my writings will be encouraged to help others through their trials. In life sometimes we cry, sometimes we laugh, and once in a while we want to scream out loud. I believe that God hears our cries, even our most quiet whisper. Sometimes our trials can feel devastating. When all is said and done, God's plan is perfect. I write to inspire hope, faith, love and courage.

Website: rebecca-robinson.org